PATRIN

PATRIN

THERESA KISHKAN

MOTHER TONGUE PUBLISHING LIMITED
Salt Spring Island B.C. Canada

MOTHER TONGUE PUBLISHING LIMITED
290 Fulford-Ganges Road, Salt Spring Island, B.C. V8K 2K6, Canada
www.mothertonguepublishing.com
Represented in North America by Heritage Group Distribution.

BOOK DESIGN Setareh Ashrafologhalai
COVER PHOTO Diana Hayes
Printed on Enviro White, 100% recycled
Printed and bound in Canada.

Mother Tongue Publishing acknowledges the assistance of the Province of British Columbia through the B.C. Arts Council, and gratefully acknowledges the support of the Canada Council for the Arts, which last year invested $157 million in writing and publishing throughout Canada.Nous remercions de son soutien le Conseil des Arts du Canada, qui a investi 157$ millions de dollars l'an dernier dans les lettres et l'édition à travers le Canada.

Library and Archives Canada Cataloguing in Publication

Kishkan, Theresa, 1955-, author
Patrin / Theresa Kishkan.

ISBN 978-1-896949-51-2 (paperback)

I. Title.

PS8571.I75P38 2015 C813'.54 C2015-904405-7

for Amy Bespflug

PATRIN OR PATERAN

is the old word for the clues Roma people left for their travelling fellows—a handful of leaves or twigs tied to a tree.

The number of lives that enter our own is incalculable.

JOHN BERGER

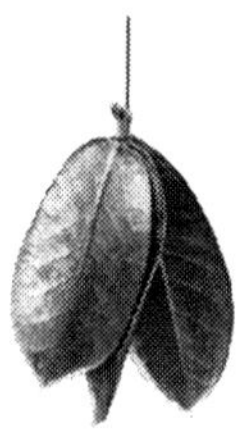

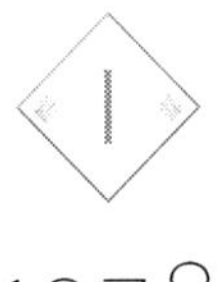

1978

WHEN I OPENED the box, the quilt released the odour of wood smoke. I let it sit in the plastic it had been wrapped in for shipping, folded and coaxed into its container. As long as I could remember, the quilt had covered my grandmother's bed.

I'd slept with her under that quilt. Four years ago, when my father died, my mother sent me to his mother for a week, and my mother arrived at the end of that week, for the mourning feast. My grandmother lived in a small house on the outskirts of Edmonton and had no extra bed. My father's room had been given over to food storage—burlap sacks of potatoes and carrots, onions hanging on strings from the ceiling, ropes of garlic, jars of plums gleaming on a shelf. Her house smelled of those things, and of woodsmoke. I don't remember if she had a furnace, but if she did, she never used it. Instead, she took her wagon (my father's childhood wagon, kept in the crawlspace under the stairs) to the trees by the river and gathered cottonwood branches brought down by wind, sawing them into stove lengths, and this was how she heated her house. Sometimes a neighbour brought over logs. My parents bought her an electric stove for cooking, but she preferred to keep a pot of stew or soup going on the wood stove. Someone gave her an occasional hare, and she had her own chickens. It was not a matter of money but the way she lived.

Those nights I slept with her, I went to bed first. I changed in the bathroom and took the side nearest the wall. She told me that she never slept an entire night through, she would have to get up to pee, and anyway she needed to feed the fire at least once before morning.

The warmth of the quilt, after the cool house, put me to sleep, and it wasn't until I felt her body against mine that I woke to the strangeness of the situation. A grandmother I hadn't seen in years, a bed she had slept in alone for four decades, my father dead. I'd just returned from a year in Europe, wandering as the young did, with a rucksack and a copy of *Europe on Ten Dollars a Day,* and I felt dislocated, adrift.

She'd named me. Patrin. It meant "leaf," my father explained, when I was old enough to wonder why I had such an odd name. My parents lived on the West Coast and hoped she would join them. But she would only visit, occasionally, and she came for my birth. Years later I wondered if she'd expected that my mother would deliver me at home, that she could stay busy boiling kettles of water and preparing a cradle. Later my father explained that, in her culture, a mother would never deliver a baby in her home, for she was considered unclean, and would stay away from the family home for 40 days before returning. In any case, she was my first visitor in the Royal Jubilee Hospital, and she was given the privilege of naming me.

I wanted to be Patty. I hated the moment when a teacher would read the class register on the first day of school and I had to raise my hand when she came to my name. Before mine, the Debbies, the Cathys. Smiths, Jacksons, Watsons. Then, a frown, a moment as she sounded my name silently before saying it aloud, always wrong: Patrin Szkandery. I wanted to die in my desk chair. I wanted so much to be a girl who didn't stand out, who had a lunch like the other lunches, not slabs of homemade bread, dark-crusted, filled with sliced eggs and sprouted alfalfa seeds. Oreos—not oatmeal cookies with raisins and walnuts. I'd raise my hand, wishing the ground would open.

And I was dark. My hair, my eyes, my skin a tone generously called olive or less charitably, swarthy. Not a girl who wore pretty dresses or patent-leather shoes. My mother shopped for quality and durability. Buster Brown saddle shoes or something she called oxfords. Plaid wool jumpers and warm sweaters. A corduroy skirt with toggle buttons I quietly cut off and said had been lost.

When my father told me it would be usual in my grandparents' country for my surname to take the feminine form—Szkanderova—I begged him not to insist on that for me. Already the teasing kept me awake at night, dreading the next day, when I'd enter the school grounds to the chant of "Szkander, Szkander, waiting for the gander," a skipping song modified to mock my name. Had I actually listened, I'd have heard "Cathy" ringing out in another cruel version, rhyming with "fatty." Or "Smith" with "piss." But a child cannot be anything but self-absorbed, particularly an only child. With a gypsy grandmother.

Her family were Kalderash; they wandered the old Austro-Hungarian Empire. Her father made superb copper vessels—there was a deep hammered pot in the Beverly house, which my grandmother took to her marriage with my grandfather, filled with her belongings; not many. His family, like hers, fled the Empire at the outset of the Great War, for different reasons, but both families sailed on the *Mount Temple* from Antwerp in 1913. My grandfather, a Catholic travelling with his brother and sister to take out homestead grants in Alberta, met my grandmother, travelling with her parents and four siblings. Her family, called Caldera in homage to their caste, kept to themselves, but somehow the young man and the young woman met and fell in love on board. By trip's end, in Saint John, they had managed a tryst or two on the unlit deck, perhaps in the shadow of lifeboats, and her parents disowned her. My grandfather thought they would relent, but he knew little of Romas and their taboos, of which he could count himself among: a gádžo. And their daughter, an unmarried girl, had been alone with a man, against the Romani chastity observances. Her father spit on her, and her mother slapped her face. She never saw them again. Her name disappeared from the family records.

Did she mind? She grieved for the rest of her life, though she was a good mother, a loving grandmother and I believe a good and loyal wife. My grandfather died 15 years into their marriage, of a lung condition related to his work as a coal miner, and she continued to raise their son on her own. My father was 13 years old when his father died.

I thought of her, her grief, her days and nights in that small house in Beverly, and then I reached into the box for her quilt, shaking it out in the privacy of my room in Victoria.

1973

WHEN I WENT to Europe, I flew from Vancouver to Spain. I don't know why Spain. It seemed like a romantic place to land. I'd never flown before, not even to a Canadian city, or across the Strait. I hoped for warmth, for bright colours and dark red wine.

When the plane landed, my backpack failed to emerge on the luggage carousel, and I didn't know what to do. I had a place to stay, a pension in Madrid someone had told me about, but I had no idea how I could proceed without my pack. I tried to speak to someone at an information desk, but I couldn't tell if she understood me or not. Unsmiling, she tapped one long-nailed finger on a pad of paper. I got to the pension somehow, went into my small room and wept. I had a guidebook, and after a short nap, I used its maps to find my way to a few of Madrid's celebrated sites. I couldn't tell you now which ones. I wandered in a fog of anxiety. I thought I should perhaps find my way to the airport and fly back to Canada. When a man who claimed he was journalist invited me for a drink, I was too unsettled by lack of sleep to accept (also by the knowledge that I hadn't changed my clothes for several days, though I had rinsed my underwear in the sink each night, hanging them on the radiator to dry). I was unsettled by the men holding machine guns outside the bank where I went to cash a traveller's cheque. Unsettled by how useless the few phrases of Spanish I'd painstakingly learned had proved.

For three mornings, I took the ticket given me by the woman who ran the pension and went next door to a cafe where I handed the ticket to a man behind a zinc counter. He looked at it, looked at me and then provided a tiny cup of coffee and two crusty rolls with a pat of butter and a dollop of marmalade on the plate. On the fourth morning, just as I was about to give up, I heard a knock and when I opened the door of my room, a man pushed my pack inside and disappeared. Maybe I'd given the woman at the airport the address of the pension or maybe the pension owner understood more of my plight than she'd let on and had followed up on my lost backpack. In any case, there it was, a bit battered. The outer pouches had been rifled through; missing were the canisters of film I'd packed and a small address book.

I had convinced myself that going home was the best thing to do, and now I had to adjust. Three days in Madrid had shown me that I wasn't particularly brave. I'd walk, and explore, but I doubted I would be the sort of traveller who found herself seamlessly absorbed into a place, who found the little bar with the brilliant guitarist, who others took into their homes and fed the food of the country at a table surrounded by interesting companions. In my jeans and brown sweater, I could have been anyone.

1978

I SHOOK OUT THE quilt. It was large, big enough for a queen-sized bed, composed of scraps of wool, mostly, though I could also identify coarse linen, a few bits and pieces of velvet, and the back of striped ticking, the kind you find on old mattresses. I think it was in fact a cover for a mattress in the Calderas' wagon, and pieced together, probably from scavenged outer edges of the bag once the central part had worn thin. A bag, roughly woven, to hold dried grass or hay, or goose feathers. The stripes had been deep blue—I could tell this by examining seams where the fabric still kept its vibrant colour, those blue stripes on a creamy background. Now both were faded almost to grey.

The wool scraps were loden, once green—again, I knew this by looking closely at the undersides of patches from which the stitching had loosened. And the velvet was black, though faded and rusty. The green wool and black velvet had been appliquéd to linen squares, the stitching fine as bird tracks, in thread now a faded yellow but once rich gold, the original colour glimpsed where stitches had been covered with sashing, now frayed. And between the squares ran sashing pieced from various lengths of grey wool.

The smell of woodsmoke and musty air. My grandmother's house. My own small flat, on the second floor of the converted theatre, had a set of double windows with a generous sill. I hung the quilt to air, leaving it for an hour or so while I rode my bike into Oak Bay Village to buy groceries. Nuts, rice and yogurt at Earth Household; carrots and apples at the Super Valu. I had enough money for a bottle of wine and chose a Hungarian red, the one with the bull on its label.

Riding back, I saw the quilt hanging from my windows like a banner. I propped my bike against the side of the building and looked up. From a distance, adjusting my eyes to its perspective, I saw the loden green scraps were leaves, scattered over the surface. Groups of two in some squares, three in others, a single leaf in many. I ran into the building, up the stairs to my apartment. I touched the densely woven fabric, a kind of felt. I bent my face to the leaves and inhaled something animal, oily. Rubbing my fingers together, it was like touching sheep, that coarse wool suffused with lanolin. My grandmother told me once that her father had worn a cloak, a loden cloak, given him by a man who'd bought some of the copper pots. It repelled both wind and rain. Sometimes he'd open it to allow two or three of his children to shelter within, she said. We sat under trees while the rain poured down, and it was our own tent, warmed by our father's body.

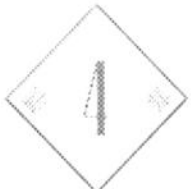

SHE HAD A garden, not tidy, but productive. Cabbages, potatoes, turnips, onions, comfrey for the chickens, runner beans, garlic. She cultivated dandelions, agrimony to flavour her hare stew, chamomile and sorrel. Everything was hung to dry from the ceiling on string or else pounded to a paste and kept in jars with oil. If I complained of stomach pains when we visited, she made a tea of chamomile, flavoured with honey. A cough meant horehound tea, bitter, even with a spoonful of sugar. She had two plum trees and sometimes made dumplings with the golden ones. She served them with sour cream and some chervil. I watched her sing to her bees one morning, not in English, and it made her seem like a character from a fairy story. But then she beat the carpets with a length of 2×4 and was herself again.

1978

I WORKED AT AN antiquarian bookstore on Fort Street, the one that advertised its hauntedness on a silk banner in the window. It didn't pay much, just a little more than minimum wage, but it was my own private library, its tall shelves and esoteric volumes a haven. Three big oak chairs, upholstered in cracked leather, provided a place to sit once I'd done the daily chores that Andrew, the owner, listed for me on a piece of paper he'd leave in the cash drawer. He spent most of his time visiting elderly people who wanted their collections appraised, and often he'd come to the shop late at night to do accounts and leave cartons of books to be unpacked. I'd let myself in each morning and turn on the dim lights, open the blinds. Some days I'd vacuum the ancient carpets laid over scarred wooden floorboards. A cat, Simpkin, lived in the store, and I'd feed him, clean out his litter box kept in the decrepit bathroom at the very back and look around for the headless corpses of mice he'd leave on the various thresholds as gifts. Thank you, Simpkin, I'd say. Good boy. He'd preen and curl himself around my legs. Then I'd shelve those books the owner had entered into the store's inventory—a series of notebooks on a shelf above the desk, one for fiction, one for history, one for autobiography—pencilling a price in the upper right-hand corner of the inner cover. And when I had finished this and no customer needed help finding a copy of Edith Wharton's *Age of Innocence,* I'd curl up in my favourite chair with whatever had caught my eye that day.

I loved the old books. Christina Rossetti, Elizabeth Gaskell, Mary Webb. Collections of poetry. And I was intrigued by the Black Sparrow books that came in regularly from someone in the city who received review copies. I hoped to be a writer myself though I had no personal models, apart from these, for what a writer might be. I wrote poetry in a notebook, typed the lines onto onionskin so I could erase anything I wanted to change more easily, and then kept these sheets in a binder I bought at Island

Blueprint on my lunch hour. I knew that plenty of poets lived in the city. I even attended readings at the various galleries and auditoriums where one or more of them would recite their poems to audiences composed largely of young people. One of the poets, a self-proclaimed witch, had noticed me in the audience, time after time, and asked if I wrote. I did. And did I have any poems to show him, he wondered. One Sunday afternoon, I cycled to his house, not far from my apartment, and he read the handful I'd brought. He made encouraging comments and asked if I'd consider joining his class at the university. He said he had an intuition about me.

My mother had hoped I'd continue my education. She wasn't happy when I travelled to Europe on my own, using the money I'd saved from the jobs after high school—working in the gift shop at Butchart Gardens, cleaning campsites in one of the provincial parks near the city. But she had my father to care for then—he'd had a heart attack and then surgery; he spent his days on the couch, his lips blue and his breathing strained— and she couldn't spend too much time worrying about me. After he died, only a month after I'd returned from my year of wandering, she sold the house I'd grown up in and went to live in an apartment off Cook Street, near Beacon Hill Park. I had dinner with her some Sundays, and she dropped into the bookstore sometimes. She'd ask carefully if I was happy. My reply was almost always the same. I'm not unhappy.

WHEN I WAS very young, we went to Edmonton every summer to visit my grandmother. We never questioned that this was the way we'd spend the two weeks of holiday time my father received from his employer, a marine communications firm. My parents owned a small trailer, which my mother spent the week before our departure readying for the journey. Bedding was aired and packed away in the storage cupboards under the seats. She made food—meatloaves, spaghetti sauce, macaroni casserole—which she froze and then put into the trailer's icebox the night before we left. This meant we didn't need to buy ice until two or three days into the trip. We meandered a bit, took our time. My father liked to fish so we spent an extra night or two at various lakes and rivers along the Yellowhead Highway where he'd get up early and try to catch our breakfast, and my mother read magazines—I remember *Redbook* and *Good Housekeeping*—in a folding lawn chair by the side of the lake, her legs turning golden brown in the sun. As advised by the magazines, she wore a hat to protect her face and prevent premature aging.

I swam. I didn't like to fish because it always seemed that the fish looked straight into my eyes as they came up on the line, panicking and thrashing to free themselves. The one time I deftly removed the hook from the throat of a fine rainbow trout and released it back into the river, my father had such a fit I thought he'd burst.

Swimming, I could forget that I was taller than most other girls my age, that I was about as unlike Hayley Mills as someone could be, and just push myself away from the shore into green water. I'd float face down as long as I could, looking at weeds and tiny bullheads, then turn to face the sun, my eyes washed clean. I had my father's skin and never burned.

I asked him questions. Did you travel here with your parents? No, he said. We had no holidays. We worked. Ever, I asked. Not ever. And were there cousins? None that I knew, though my mother came to Canada with sisters and brothers, but they had no contact. What about your father's side of the family? That's enough questions, he said, with such finality that I didn't try again.

We stopped, always, at Maligne Canyon where we looked down so far to water that I felt dizzy, felt like the planet had tilted and I had lost my gravity. After that, it was a morning's drive to Edmonton, with one stop at Edson for ice cream and somewhere else to eat meatloaf sandwiches before we arrived. My mother poured coffee from the dented silver thermos for my father and for herself, and I had lemonade from the jar she kept in the icebox.

Once we'd arrived, my father backed the trailer into the weedy driveway next to the small house he'd grown up in, and my mother took her gift of apples and peaches into my grandmother's kitchen, which smelled of her—wool and smoke and something she rubbed into her knees when they ached.

1978

ONCE I'D AIRED the quilt, I wondered about repairs. The edges of some of the leaves were frayed beyond their stitching. I could tuck the frayed ends under, press them, I thought, and then whipstitch them again. The binding was worn thin. In places it had vanished, letting the sides gape. I could go down to Capital Iron and find fabric to cut into long strips for new binding. I knew of other places to buy fabric, but I loved Capital Iron. The buildings, two of them, were connected by a walkway, and I loved the wide rough boards on the floors, the stairs, the piles of jeans and Army surplus shorts, fishing rods and enamelled coffee pots with wire handles for hanging on a stick over a campfire. The fabric section had bins of remnants, rolled into compact tubes with paper labels providing the dimensions, a price. I'd found curtain material there for the bathroom window of my apartment, and I hoped to buy a remnant of grey wool, which I thought would make a good replacement binding for my grandmother's quilt.

Who had made it in the first place? She told me that her mother had quietly put it in the copper pot she carried away from the dock in Saint John, after her mother had slapped her face and her father had cut the coins from her hair with his sharp knife. So she would go out into the world of the gádžo with a hammered pot, a quilt and the mark of her mother's hand on her cheek.

So did *her* mother make the quilt? My great-grandmother? I laid it out on my bed to see what other repairs might be necessary. Whose hand had stitched the leaves, had cut the sashing that ran between each square, most of it grey flannel, like men's trousers, some of the lengths pieced together? And where did the velvet come from, the nap as soft as a cat's stomach? My grandmother disliked cats. She said they were unclean, that they washed their own anuses and used their own paws to bury their faeces. She had the dog, in later years, to protect her hens, but she didn't love it—a mixed breed that lived in the yard and slept on hay she kept by the entrance to her crawlspace. She fed it bones so cleaned of any meat or gristle that the dog's only nourishment came from cracking open the bones for the marrow. Fish someone brought her from the Saskatchewan River, whiskered and pallid. And sometimes, on very cold nights, she gave the dog a pan of old bread soaked in warm broth. She wasn't cruel, but practicality came first.

SHE USED CHICORY in her coffee, long roots she dug by the roadside, then dried on strings hanging near her wood stove. She roasted them and ground them to add to precious coffee, measured out with a brass scoop. I loved the smell, and how she brought me a cup at first light, that week I stayed with her—the luxury of having someone bring me coffee in bed, the smoky quilt pulled up to my shoulders as I leaned back against my pillow, the window frosty inside and out. A tiny bird searched for insects around the window frame.

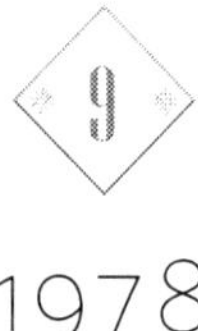

1978

MY MOTHER SAID, Your great-grandmother made the quilt for your grandmother's dowry, and that's why she was able to take it with her in Saint John. Or that's what she told me. And she had so little to leave anyone, but she wanted you to have it. I gave the copper bucket to her neighbour, the one who helped her. But she had already packed the quilt up in a box, with an envelope taped to it with enough money to mail it. Her wishes were clear.

Do you know anything else about her? My great-grandmother, I mean?

No, not much. Your grandmother told me once that her mother hadn't wanted to leave Europe because several of her babies were buried there. So much disease in those years, illnesses we have treatments for now. Even measles could kill a child, not to mention whooping cough or diphtheria. And those children living in a wagon, camping in tents in all weather—it doesn't bear thinking about, does it?

But I couldn't stop thinking about her. Them. I found charcoal grey flannel at Capitol Iron, enough to cut into strips, to piece carefully to the required lengths and then press with a damp cloth to make binding. I didn't have a sewing machine but neither had the woman who made the quilt. She probably didn't even have a room but worked by an outdoor fire, or in a tent or in a wagon. Her life would have been as different from mine as a life could be, yet we were related. When I looked at the way she'd sewn on the loden leaves, I knew something about her hands. How she must have smoothed out the edges of each green scrap, arranging it, threading a needle in daylight or firelight and making those impossibly small even stitches.

I pinned new strips over the worn binding. I knew that the corners would be a challenge. My great-grandmother had mitered her corners, but I wasn't sure I could do that neatly. Perhaps I would simply wrap the strips around each corner and ease my stitching to allow a curve.

Running the needle in and out, drawing the thread through all those layers—six, including the batting, which seemed to be an old blanket—should have been difficult, but the fabric was mostly so thin that I hardly needed to push. I had a thimble, but I didn't require it, except for one or two areas where the old binding remained intact. I pinned and stitched and unpinned and smoothed. The strip of grey flannel slowly fastened the top of the quilt to the underside, closing the gap. I was adding a hinge, it felt like—a hinge between my great-grandmother and her daughter, my grandmother and myself. It opened to the past. It let me be the gate between two women, one in Central Europe, one in

Edmonton, who hadn't spoken for more decades than they could have imagined in the years when one of them sewed in a clearing near the Slovak border, sewing for the one who would be banished from her heart, that one still a child twirling under the trees in her long colourful skirt.

SHE COULDN'T READ or write when she arrived in Canada. Most gypsies couldn't. But when my father went to school, she went too, sitting in a small desk in the primary classroom, learning to decode the marks that made up the alphabet. She didn't continue after she'd learned the basics of reading and writing. She never intended to do more reading than was necessary but wanted the ability to read documents and write lists, to fill out forms with confidence. My grandfather was illiterate too and only learned to print his name, taught by my father. Maybe that was at the heart of my father's anger when I asked too many questions. The distance between us, between now and that time—my father afraid I'd make assumptions based on my literacy and their lack of it, my privilege and their poverty. But I wanted so desperately to know them.

As a child, I wrote letters to my grandmother from Victoria. Keep it simple, my father advised, and I did. I illustrated my words with little drawings—our new dog, my mother's garden, a robins' nest in our apple tree with three eggs inside (from the upper window, with binoculars, I could look right into the nest without bothering the parents). I thanked her for her gifts of ribbons and once, after I'd had my ears pierced in grade eight, a pair of golden hoops. Those were hers, my father said, holding them in the palm of his hand. She never took them out of her ears. You must take very good care of them. I drew myself, with the hoops safe at home in each ear.

I sent postcards when I went to Europe. Even without my stolen address book, I knew where to send them: 3846-111 Avenue, Edmonton, Alberta. Gaudi's strange buildings in Barcelona, the Sistine Chapel in Rome, a man dressed in traditional Cretan clothing riding a donkey. What did she make of them, these images from a continent she'd fled as a girl? In those years, it was difficult to get visas for Communist countries, so I didn't even try to go to Czechoslovakia, the nearest thing she had to a motherland. But in truth, her family had no true country. They wandered, sometimes with a kumpania, sometimes alone. Her father worked for periods for a rich landowner in Moravia-Silesia, in the area now called Czechoslovakia, but then it was part of the empire ruled by the Hapsburgs. She told me once that her father could work any metal, not just copper, and he'd spent a winter repairing wheels, shoeing horses, making gates and ornate iron structures for the landowner's gardens. The family was given a small house to live in while he worked. Perhaps some of the quilt fabrics had come from there—clothing passed down for the children, my great-grandmother adjusting items to fit them, scraps kept and used for the quilt. The black velvet, some small pieces of brocade, the linen squares themselves.

So much unknown, so much to surmise. The warm weight of a quilt across my lap as I sewed and repaired made sad compensation for all that I could never know.

1978

I WAS SWEEPING THE area just outside the bookstore entrance when the poet appeared. He seemed startled to see me there.

I'm looking for a copy of the *Carmina Gadelica,* he said. And I went inside to check the shelves. I recognized the title but hadn't remembered that we had all six volumes, though in different editions, most bound in red cloth over boards, with gilt titles on the spines. I took down the volumes, placed them on a table by one of the leather armchairs, and asked him if he would like a cup of tea.

I remember this very edition, he exclaimed, his eyes ecstatic as he examined one of the red-bound volumes. The library at my university in England had it. I spent hours reading these. He opened at random. His rich voice incanted:

WELL can I say my rune,
Descending with the glen;
One rune,
Two runes,
Three runes,
Four runes,
Five runes,
Six runes.
Seven runes,
Seven and a half runes,
Seven and a half runes.
May the man of this clothing never be wounded,
May torn he never be;
What time he goes into battle or combat,
May the sanctuary shield of the Lord be his.
What time he goes into battle or combat,
May the sanctuary shield of the Lord be his.
This is not second clothing and it is not thigged,
Nor is it the right of sacristan or of priest.
Cresses green culled beneath a stone,
And given to a woman in secret.
The shank of the deer in the head of the herring,
And in the slender tail of the speckled salmon.

I've never heard anything like that, I told him.

He explained that the volumes contained poems, blessings, charms and other lore collected in the late 19th century by a folklorist, Alexander Carmichael, in the remote parts of Scotland. Everything from blessings for milk cows to love charms and fertility spells could be found in those pages. Carmichael visited Gaelic-speaking communities and asked for stories and songs. He edited the first few volumes, and the rest came out over the years as others finished his work after his death. How much does the set cost?

Nearly $500, I whispered, looking at volume one for the pencilled price. $495. Firm, in Andrew's small neat script. A file card noted that all the volumes must be sold together. I couldn't imagine anyone agreeing to pay that much for six old books. Yet, that poem had echoed . . .

Very well. I'll write a cheque, said the poet.

Could you find that one again that you just read, I asked him. And he did—a consecration for cloth. The last stanza . . . *Cresses green culled beneath a stone,/And given to a woman in secret.* I felt as though I was being spoken to, personally, across the decades. Before wrapping the books for him, I copied out the lines.

When you're ready, come to my class, the poet said as he left.

1973

AFTER SPAIN, I'D gone by train to Italy, but I didn't stop there, apart from changing trains in Rome for one bound for Brindisi. I wanted the sun, and I wanted what waited for me in Greece, on Crete: a chance to be the person I'd always hoped to be. A poet, a young woman whose dark looks would blend in, whose odd name would no longer set her apart.

The ferry sailed by night from Brindisi to Piraeus. The stars hung low enough to touch, to wish on, and I confess I wished for love. No boy had ever paid attention to me. I attended no dances in high school, no parties. As the ferry moved through the Gulf of Corinth, at dawn, I watched dolphins in the turquoise waters.

And another ferry to Crete, where I tried to sleep while all around me goats bleated, chickens clucked until someone finally put a blanket over their basket, and a man played strangely beautiful melodies on a pear-shaped instrument he cradled in his arms like a sleeping child. His own child leaned against him, her arm across her eyes. Rough red wine was handed around, and I drank deeply, thirsty for whatever would come.

Do you like it? A man stood next to the seat where I'd been trying to doze off. He gestured towards the player who had finished a song and now simply strummed the strings. Not Greek, eh? He pronounced it "Grik."

No, I'm not Greek. But yes, it's wonderful. What's that instrument called?

A lyra. Comes from Crete, but you'll find them all over Greece. Other parts of Europe too. The first ones were made from tortoise shells! He threw back his head and laughed. He had an accent. Was he Greek himself?

Macedonian. Ah, don't ask what that means. It means everything, and nothing. And my mother is Roma so I am a kind of nothing too. Part tsiganoi, which is what they call us in Greece. But I am a musician and that's something! He was still laughing as he drew a long horn out of a velvet bag he removed from his rucksack. You don't know what this is?

A question, but he was sure of the answer. How could I know? He blew slightly, and it made a deep and beautiful sound. A zurna, he said, stroking its length. Made of apricot wood. A bit loud, maybe, for inside. Let's go out, and I'll play you a welcome to Greece.

On the deck, the horn sounded loud and lonely. Some others gathered to listen. A sky spangled with stars, the eerie moan of air passing through apricot wood. I could have listened all night.

Hey, I'm Nestor by the way. And you?

Patrin.

Patrin? He looked closely at me, and then looked again. He said a few words in the language my grandmother had used but I couldn't understand. I must've looked blank. You're Roma?

My grandmother was, and she got to name me. It means, like, leaves? And can you tell? The Roma part, I mean?

Leaves, yes, but more than that. It's the sign left by travellers for others to follow. Leaves sometimes, or sticks, or pieces of cloth tied to a tree. He used his hands when he talked, giving me the shape of the leaves, the image of the sticks, the act of tying cloth to a tree. Only those that the message was left for would know how to read it. And yes, the Roma always know another. But, hey, it's usually a boy's name. And you're not a boy! A long appraising look that felt as warm as sunlight on my bare skin.

By the time we got to Heraklion, just as the sun rose, he'd invited me to join him for a few days in Chania, where he would play some gigs and teach a short course. He had a small old Deux Chevaux, red, with a canvas roof. With a little work, we managed to fit in my backpack. I held the zurna in its velvet bag.

1978

THE POEM ABOUT cloth insinuated its way into my work with the quilt. *Cresses green culled beneath a stone,/And given to a woman in secret./The shank of the deer in the head of the herring,/And in the slender tail of the speckled salmon.* Was it a code? I knew about watercress and how it grew in cold clean water. How it could refresh water with its filtering root system. Did a secret reside in the loden green leaves, the small elegant scraps of velvet?

The new binding made the quilt look more finished. More durable somehow. By the time I'd worked my way around the second side, with two left to go, my stitches had become more regular. I felt guided by the quilt's maker. She had not hurried with this covering. She couldn't have hurried. The pattern contained too many elements, too much work, and I suspected that the days of a Roma woman at the turn of the 20th century would not have allowed for much leisure. I could smell tallow and lamp oil, now part of the fibres, so some of her sewing must have been done in the evenings. I recognized these odours from my grandmother's house: for years she begged suet from the local butcher and made her own candles from the rendered fat, sweetened with bees' wax. So I smelled her candles, her mother's candles, and the lamp oil from the wagon and from her own small house.

I kept notes of my progress, careful tallies of the squares I'd repaired, the time it took me to stitch my strips of grey flannel over the disintegrating binding. Without really intending to, my lines echoed the consecration for cloth from the *Carmina Gadelica.*

Green leaves on grey ground, dark velvet, the textures of night, shadows, gold thread the lines of light coming through trees, bird tracks at dawn. Where did she get the brocade? Who lost their bed for the ticking? Their blanket for the batting? Did she sew by day, with horses in the background, tied to the wagons? Or by night, someone crooning a ballad in the darkness beyond the fire?

I cycled to the poet's house and asked if I could attend his class. He occasionally invited guests to a poetry workshop to share work with the students if he thought that person would benefit from the experience. Would it matter that I hadn't paid tuition, I wondered. He'd been teaching so long, he said, that he could do almost anything he wanted.

I didn't know much about the shaping of a poem, though I'd written them for years. I'd never thought about form. I had the words, the images for this one, but I hadn't known how to put them together on the page so they would read the way I wanted them to, and it seemed important this time to explore that relationship—white space and black letters. I experimented a little before the workshop and ended up with something that looked like this.

Green leaves on
        grey ground, dark velvet, these textures of night,
shadows, gold thread, lines coming
        through the trees.
Birdtracks at dawn.
Where did she get the brocade?
Who traded copper for linen,
wool for silk?
Who lost their bed for the ticking?
Their blanket for the batting?
Did she sew by day,
        horses in the background,
        tied
        to the wagons?
Or by night, someone crooning

a ballad in the darkness
            beyond the fire?
Who lost their bed?

The students in the workshop were all younger than me. So assured, so confident, their poems handed around in multiple copies made on something called a Banda machine that they used in a room by the office; it produced as many copies as needed, in strong-smelling purple ink. The idea was that a person read his or her poem and the others offered suggestions to improve it. They used terms I'd never heard before—assonance, ellipsis, the breath line. And how easily they could say to someone who had passed around a sheet: Well, the real poem begins here—pointing to a line halfway down the page. I didn't utter a word. I wouldn't have known what to say in the first place, and in the second, their reading skills and their facility with language terrified me.

The poet introduced me. I had only one copy of my poem so I simply read it. My voice trembled. They asked to hear it again. The second time I read better. Someone asked to see it "on the page" which I realized meant that he—a young man wearing a beret and several scarves around his neck—wanted to look at the copy I'd brought.

Others commented that they couldn't isolate an anchor, the central metaphor, how would I define the tenor, could I discuss my use of metonymy vis-à-vis the bed, and did I consider the poem to be a lyric or a narrative. I couldn't speak. But the young man with the beret read my poem aloud, in an accent I couldn't identify, and said that it was entirely its own thing, its own form, more like a spell than anything else. The language was heightened to the point of being incantatory, he said. I listened and made notes. The poet leading the workshop smiled and nodded.

Thank you, my dear, he said as the class ended. That was a gift. But all I knew was that I couldn't return.

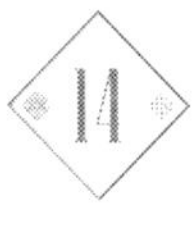

1973

NESTOR HAD A friend who had a flat in one of the old Venetian palaces by the harbour in Chania. Looking out the great windows, you saw boats, and the azure sea. The ancient lighthouse or Faros, Yiannis called it. Yiannis taught at the Venizelian Conservatory of Music, specializing in Cretan folk instruments and music. He'd invited Nestor to give a short course, two weeks in length, on the zurna, along with a lyra player and someone who played the hang drum. Another man had a collection of ntaoulaki, ancient drums from eastern Crete. Together, these guys would explore the Cretan songs collected by a musicologist at the Conservatory, adapting and extending the potentials for harmony, in the context of sharing technique with the students.

Nestor told me privately that the lyra and zurna did not work together. The zurna was one of ta organa: the instruments. Two zurnas could play together (the protos, or lead melodist, and the passadoros, or drone player), partnered with the dauli or bass drum. They are a family all their own, and they don't like others, he said, and grinned. But we will play together, these guys and me, and see what happens.

Yiannis assumed we were a couple. He showed us to a large bare room, furnished only with a bed, its frame elaborately carved from fragrant wood, its bedding coarse sheets and a coverlet of the bright Cretan shepherd's weave, still smelling of sheep's wool. The balcony contained a geranium in an olive oil tin and a small table with two chairs.

I'd like to say that I entered that bed casually, the way a young woman who'd come of age in the late 1960s would have done, slipping naked between the sheets, her hair cascading down her shoulders. But I was as innocent of men as was possible. I wore a T-shirt and underpants to bed, and he said, Is that what you wear to seduce a man? I replied, I have no idea how to seduce a man.

Ah, Patrin, he said, holding my face between his hands. You have no idea. That's what you tell me. But you are so beautiful that men must trail behind you, begging you to allow them to worship you.

I think he was joking. But he kissed my forehead and said, We'll wait until we know each other better. And then he tucked me in, like my mother used to, with the strong-smelling coverlet softened by a turn of the top sheet. Sweet dreams, my leaf.

I explored the city while he taught his classes at the Odeion. The classes overflowed to a bar afterwards, not one of the fancy ones on the harbour, but a smoky room down a narrow lane, the window hung with saddlebags, and a courtyard, turned inward, with metal tables clustered around a vine. It wasn't far from Yiannis's flat so he stopped for me on his way there, saying, You'll hear some of the true music tonight.

How to describe that music? Some of it made me want to dance, and certainly people danced; mostly men, as dancing was a particularly male activity on Crete. The door stood open, and they moved inside and out as though the two were the same place. Two zurnas and a dauli, out under the vine. The sound filled the darkness right down to the harbour where the water answered back. Some songs I knew must be rebel songs for their ferocity, the way the older men at the bar raised their fists and loudly sang the refrains. But other songs, plangent and achingly lovely, entered my body and made me feel intense sorrow—though I didn't know what to attach the sorrow to. Yiannis, beside me, told me that Nestor brought the gypsy soul to Cretan music, played the zurna with a gypsy inflection. The long quavering notes, rich with vibrato—the other musicians stopped playing to listen. I was unused to wine, and my glass kept being refilled. Piney, and sharp, it was a perfect accompaniment to the salty cheese and the plates of small fried fish, tomatoes coated with golden oil, dishes of olives, green and black, some of them bitter and others as large and meaty as chicken. Loaves of bread, heavy, dusty with flour. When we finally found our way back to the flat, trailed by a few young men who wanted to know, How do you make the reeds? How do you know what to give to the drone player? Nestor told them, Tomorrow, ask me tomorrow. I must take this young lady to her bed.

That night he unbraided my hair and put a towel under my naked body—tonight, kardia mou, do not wear your T-shirt. Although I can't say it was perfect—the next morning I hurt all over—I learned that there are ways of forgetting where your own body ends and another's begins, that the flesh feels beautiful, not marked or calloused; it yearns to be fused to the flesh of the beloved. For already I thought of him that way. He had made love to me with his music and then his body. Every inch of my body was imprinted with his, a leaf in clay.

After the third time we made love, I knew what the songs were about. I had grown up, at last. The warmth, the tingling, the way he made my body vibrate with his mouth. I would turn to him in the morning, hungry. He was more than willing to feed me. The riches of his body made me full, briefly, and then I was ravenous again. Sunlight, intense and dry, on bare skin. I knew how this would feel.

Where did you learn your English?

In New York. I spent five years playing with other musicians. Roma live there too you know. Everywhere it seems. Even Edmonton, you tell me.

He played the zurna on the terrace, a piercing call to life. It could be one thing one moment—a plaintive horn, turning in on itself, finding a road inward; then it would wail, cry out and wake the sleeping city. When church bells rang, he found a way to harmonize, to bend the notes and make them shudder. For me, it felt like a perfect meal, gorgeous and filling.

He took me to little villages in the mountains when he heard a rumour of a song, a musician, and there'd be the ceremony of water, a spoon of quince jam, and then raki coming out on the table while someone found a shepherd who played a homemade flute, who sang in a rough voice. Who smelled of his flock. The man would begin a tune, and Nestor would listen briefly, his hand tapping his knee, then he would take up his zurna and play along.

You don't write down the notes? I asked him, after one of these meetings, and he said, No, no, I just listen.

On a Saturday, he said, I am going to buy you a dress. No more this brown sweater, these jeans. A woman like you should be robed in something beautiful.

We visited a stall with women's clothing—blouses cut in the Minoan style, long skirts and a few dresses in vivid colours trimmed with gold ribbon. He chose one, with a full skirt cut on the bias, in ultramarine blue. Try this. The woman has a little curtained place behind her, just there. Try it and show me.

I put on the lovely dress and stepped out, in bare feet, for my hiking boots seemed too clumsy to wear under this confection. I twirled, self-consciously, but I loved how the skirt flowed as I turned. Oh, yes, he said. You are beautiful, and the dress is what you will wear. I will buy it, kardia mou.

He bartered with the woman, laughing with her as they agreed on a price and waited while she wrapped it in brown paper. And now for boots.

I can't let you . . .

You can do nothing to stop me, he replied. He took me by the hand and led me to another of the narrow lanes leading away from the harbour, to a narrow shop, its window hung with skins.

He took me inside. In rapid Greek, he indicated a skin, a deep golden brown, and the man unhooked it from the window. Nestor examined it. The man traced my bare feet on a piece of newspaper, measured my calves with a piece of string, and then made a gesture with his hand, five fingers raised.

In five days, you will have boots, said Nestor, as we went back to the flat for lunch.

1978

THE LODEN LEAVES fell in a pattern, I realized. Their placement wasn't random, though the eye at first expected geometry and this pattern was something else. I made a little drawing to try to work out the design. A little drawing, a poem: *a ballad in the darkness.*

1973

AND THEN it was over.

He told me that he had to return to Macedonia—some gigs, family business, a wedding. You know our Roma weddings! They go on for a week! I waited. Would he invite me to come with him? No, he didn't. The course was finished, he was gathering up his clothing and the cassettes of music he'd accumulated during the two weeks in Chania. The small table on the balcony still held the remains of our breakfast—half a brown loaf, that thyme-scented honey, yogurt bought in a store that also sold strong cheeses made from the milk of island sheep, as was this yogurt, thick and rich. A tiny copper briki in which coffee had been boiled three times. Tall glasses of cool water.

He stopped packing to tell me how much he'd enjoyed the past two weeks, that I was lovely, that I would do great things, that...

No, I said. Don't. And I began to cry. He put his hands on my shoulders, but I shook them off. Don't. I'm fine. I don't know why I'm crying. I have other plans too. I gathered up my own belongings as quickly as I could—the beautiful dress, my journal, two pairs of underpants drying on the radiator. I tied my new boots to the pack frame. And I put my old boots on, telling him it was best for me to disappear. Whoosh. Look away and I'll be gone.

Let me take you to the bus station at least. And I'd like us to stay in touch. He wrote his address on a page torn from his notebook, but I didn't pick it up.

Thank you for the boots, I said. I grabbed my backpack, boots swinging, took one last look at the balcony. He followed me for a few minutes, saying, We should talk, please don't go away angry, but when I ran, he turned back.

A tiny copper briki in which coffee had been boiled. Tall glasses of cool water. Out of time, a moment, like a painting I carried in my heart.

1974

THOSE NIGHTS I slept with her, I went to bed first. My father's death made me cold. And Edmonton, in late April, was leafless and grim. There'd been a snowfall, then another; then the snow disappeared while we slept, vanishing into thin air, cold air. But any green had turned brown or worse. I performed errands for my grandmother, walking many blocks with a list she'd written out with many pauses and deliberations: to the butcher who saved bones for her, and to the market for rice, the five-pound bag if that wasn't too heavy for me to carry? Milk—she felt I should have milk. But how much would I need? A quart? Two quarts? If she had milk, she would make borscht a Doukhobor woman had brought for her once, all vegetables and butter and cream, with only one beet, which surprised her because the Ukrainians in the neighbourhood made theirs with beets and vinegar and thin slices of beef. I used some of my own money to buy two tins of dog food. I knew she'd scold me, but I wanted the dog to have some pleasure. I asked if I could take him with me, on a lead, but she said, No, because then he would expect it in the future and you wouldn't be there to take him. No point in setting him up for disappointment.

While I walked, I thought about my father. He'd been weak for so long that his death wasn't really a surprise, though it hurt me to realize that we'd never have the kind of conversations I'd wanted all my life. Sometimes he'd tell me bits and pieces, scraps, and sometimes he'd tell me that it was none of my business when I asked about his childhood.

I wanted to cry out, How will I know who I am if I don't know who you were? But I knew he would turn his head away at such a thought, and my mother would be cross with me for upsetting him.

I was cold, those nights. My grandmother's house was drafty, though I could sit near the wood stove with a book, and the side of me closest to the fire would stay toasty and warm. I'd hear my grandmother chopping some dried plant to make a tea for sleep or pain or digestion. Some of her teas smelled enticing—with chamomile or mint or the sage she dried in great bunches like brooms. And some smelled strange or bitter. Valerian, rue, agrimony, milk thistle. Sometimes she gave me a cup of sage tea to sip while I sat in bed, propped up with my pillow, and hers. I wore my big woollen work socks with flannel pajamas. The weight of the quilt and the heat of the tea made me sleepy enough to set my cup on the windowsill and slide down into dreaming. Once I dreamed of my father in this very house, a boy working at a table with an oil lamp illuminating his copybook, his pencil, as he wrote the story of his life, which had ended, and I woke, wishing for that copybook to read by the river while leaves dropped from the cottonwoods and aspens and ducks muttered on the water.

I blamed myself for losing Nestor through inexperience. Maybe if I'd known more about men. But it was also love—on my part at least. I loved his voice, his laugh, the rough skin of his elbows. I loved waking to someone next to me. I loved that he called me kardia mou, my heart. I loved his interest in me—what I thought, what I wrote in my journal, who my parents were, how much Romani I spoke. Almost none, but I knew a few words, the ones my grandmother used to express anger, or pleasure. Bogacha: her exclamation when she took her dense brown loaves from the oven. My chey, she called me: my girl. And lashav, she'd shout at the boys who teased her dog. For shame, for shame! And her sorrow when she realized that I would not be present for all the pomana, the feasts of remembrance, she would cook for my father after his death, each according to ritual: one at forty days, another at six months, the last at a year. I stayed for the first, seven days after his death, along with my mother. Three of us mourning was better than two; an even number would have meant bad luck. We had pastry fried in oil, a ring of it, with a candle in the middle. We said a prayer:

Te primin le mulekhê o Del e pomana kadja, aj te xan la źuvindi!
"God, this pomana shall be for this dead, eat!"

And after the meal, we took the remains of the pastry to the river and threw it as far as we could into the dark water. Then my mother drove me to the airport in the rented car, and I returned to Victoria. My mother remained in Edmonton to settle my father's affairs and to ease my grandmother into the next phase of her life, one with neither a husband—she was used to that, though she never ceased to wear black, in recognition—nor a son.

I thought of her with her bowl of soup, her candle, my father's photograph on the table. When I phoned her after the second pomana, she expressed relief that a bee had entered the room while she ate her meal alone, one person, an uneven number. It meant my father was on his way to the Kingdom of the dead, maybe already eating the linden flower honey she remembered from home. Nothing in this country compared.

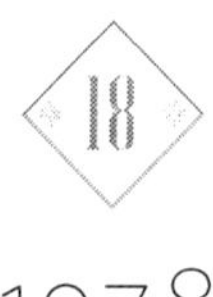

1978

AT FIRST I thought of them as simply green leaves. Leaves of loden wool. But then I saw the differences. In one square, four oak leaves. They were so obviously oak leaves—I lived in a city with oak trees everywhere, beautiful Garry oaks, and although I knew that other kinds of oaks existed without the characteristic deeply round-lobed leaves of *Quercus garryana,* these were recognizably oaks.

In another square, three cordate or heart-shaped leaves sweeping away from their stalk. I consulted a field guide at the bookstore and learned that they were linden leaves. And another square held five long leaves with crenate margins, lightly toothed. On two of them hung husks, which I supposed contained nuts, and looking closely I could see the remains of stitching, which suggested bristles. These leaves and husks most closely resembled beech leaves with cupules containing the triangular edible nuts, though they contained a lot of tannin and had to be leached, then formed into cakes, or mast, which was actually quite palatable. I learned that the genus name, *Fagus,* meant "to eat" in Greek, so perhaps people who lived as my great-grandmother lived would have considered beech nuts important as food. For their animals if not for themselves.

And then a single leaf, a maple. When I looked in the field guide to see what maples grew in Central Europe, I found one named

Acer pseudoplatanus, the sycamore maple; its specific name alluded to its resemblance to the plane tree, though the two weren't related, or maybe just distantly. I remembered the plane trees growing in town squares all over Europe. And this maple was noted for the honey produced from the nectar of its flowers and its beautiful wood, used for the necks, scrolls and backs of violins. The wavy grain of the wood often resulted in handsome veneers.

My grandmother kept bees. She made their hives from coarse rye grass, which she wove into acorn-shaped baskets, skeps, she called them, sewn together with rough string. She kept them in small alcoves she built into the side of her house, and in the fall, she fearlessly removed the honeycombs, waving a smoky torch to make the bees sleepy. This honey was her main source of sweetener, and when I was a child, I loved finding a small section of comb on my plate, to eat with toasted slices of her dense bread, the honey strongly flavoured because she grew so many medicinal herbs in her garden.

1973

I HAD NO IDEA where to go. But I got on a bus; the rear-view mirror held a tangle of beads, rosaries and little ikons hanging from leather thongs. I rode that bus to Chora Skafion, the end of the line.

I found a room. I didn't know that I should barter, but it seemed so cheap; I was happy to pay the price the woman in black wrote carefully onto the back of a cigarette box. The room had two beds and a small balcony with iron railings painted bright blue. I hung my clothes in the wooden wardrobe—my dress, my extra pair of jeans.

No one knew where I was, no one could find me. I climbed to the hills above the village each day, sitting on rocks while my heart crouched like a dark animal in my thorax. If I could have held it tenderly in my hands, blown softly in its ear, told it the pain would go, just relax, be sweet to yourself, I would have. The air was pine-scented, and from time to time, I'd hear bells. Bells? Turning, I saw goats bounding over the rocks, in search of grass and strong herbs. Some of them had slender curved horns. One came quite close, its eyes so strange that I couldn't stop looking. Golden, the pupils dark and almost rectangular. It had a strong odour, pushing its face towards me, tufts of dry grass threaded through its beard. I saw myself in the black mirror at the centre of its eye, a young woman heavy with sadness. I touched its head, the hair coarse as burlap. It gave a bleat, a yelp, and ran back to its tribe.

Alone again, I thought, I could stay here forever among the rocks, listening to bees and the bells of the goats. I'd watch the sun set night after night over Africa, a few boats making their slow way home to port. When I slept, one hand on the big stone that anchored me, the goats might come again, in moonlight, to nibble at my hair. And after I died, the long bones of my ribs would crumble to dust.

Wilder goats, their horns longer and more elegant, swept back from their heads, sometimes followed the belled goats, and once I watched one of these mount a bell-wearing goat, thrusting himself into her body while she uttered a plaintive cry. The herd moved on without her until, released by her captor, she ran on her delicate legs to join them again, her tail twitching dismissively.

I wasn't hungry and didn't bother to eat. It was such a small village: someone must have mentioned to my landlady that I hadn't shopped in the tiny store or eaten at the single taverna because when I returned from my walk on my third day, I found a dish of olives, several slices of brown bread, cucumber, three oranges and a piece of salty white cheese waiting for me in my room. I sat on the balcony and realized that everything tasted delicious and that no man could be worth starving for, not even one with a zurna of apricot wood. That evening, I put on my dress and boots and went to the taverna for a glass of retsina and a bowl of bean soup. The music that night sounded wonderful; a bouzouki player sat in a corner and played tunes that matched the sky; the Libyan Sea eased itself to the shore, then receded. No one spoke to me, but I felt involved somehow—with life, with music, with the small lizard scuttling up the trunk of a magenta bougainvillea by the door to the taverna.

When I returned to my room, I made notes in my journal, trying to find language for how I felt. A goat met me on the rocks above the village, its breath grass and thyme. In its eyes, the courtyard outside the taverna in Chania, in its eyes the oblong of bed looking out to Faros. Bees in the celandine, the red poppies, prickly gorse, daisies holding the sun in their centres. I hold my hand to the goat and hear bells, the faint sound of Nestor rubbing my body with oil, the rough pumice of his hands.

1978

I SMOOTHED THE GREEN leaves with the tip of my finger. Some of the wool had worn away completely so I used a fine needle to stitch the edges of what fabric remained in place. How tiny the original stitches, in that thread that had once been rich yellow. I followed the veins of the leaves, their delicate branching. In brocade, the sound of leaves rustling in wind, turning their silver backs to the sky.

The quilt lay on my bed, and some mornings I sat up with a cup of coffee on the little table, sewing in place. Sewing the leaves my great-grandmother had created on linen, a Roma woman nearly a century before, in a country I'd never seen, with children around her, one of whom was my grandmother, and the others great-aunts and uncles I'd never know. Somewhere one horse called to another. Rain fell on the wagon and splashed from trees. The fire sizzled.

The telephone rang, a loud sound in my quiet rooms. Hardly anyone phoned me. My mother, the man who owned the bookshop, asking, Could you open early on Saturday for a customer with limited time, or Do you remember who had bought the signed first edition of Grainger, because someone else is willing to pay a lot of money? But this was the poet, the one who'd invited me to his class. This time he invited me to a party.

A party! What would I wear? All I owned that was remotely fancy was the dress from the Chania market. I hadn't worn it for at least two years. Would it fit? It did. And my Greek boots, cleaned and rubbed with dubbin to make them glow. I had a necklace I'd bought at a street market in Florence, and I braided my hair. There. That was the best I could do. A bottle of Bull's Blood to take as an offering.

The poet greeted me at the door, soundly kissing each cheek. He led me into his house by the hand, taking me to say hello to his wife, a large generous woman who embraced me like an old friend. When I'd cycled over before, to ask if I could attend his poetry class, she'd brought tea to where we sat in the poet's untidy study. Welcome, she said then, and now.

What a house. It stood on a corner lot, imposing in its size and age, in a city not known for history, or at least history I knew. A large entrance hall opened into two rooms made one by the opening of double French doors. Although I'd been there before, the house felt different, noisy and alive with festivity. A fire snapped in the grate, and so many people stood about I wondered if I should quietly let myself out again.

But I didn't. I accepted a glass of wine and stood below a painting, which I studied as long as I could to avoid feeling that I was the only person without someone else to talk to. I'd never been in a house with so many paintings. They weren't arranged one to a wall, all at the same height, but hung wherever a patch of wall made room for them. And objects jostled for room on every surface—little carvings, pottery sculptures, animals made of wire. A trio of women so beautiful I thought of them as the Three Graces drank and laughed by the fireplace, attracting most of the men to them like bees to bright blooms. But soon a man appeared at my elbow also. He had a German accent.

He commented on my dress, my face, the angle of my shoulder. As an artist, it was his job to notice such details, he said. After two glasses of wine (he refilled my glass once I'd finished the first), I told him about my job at the bookstore while he fixed his eyes on my face as I talked. I excused myself to use the toilet—a room filled with more paintings and a bookshelf, the first I'd ever seen in a bathroom. When I returned to the party, I politely removed the hand of a rheumy-eyed elderly man who had clamped it on my bum with a surprising sense of direction. The artist was undressing by the fire and singing a song in German. Some people watched and clapped, but most simply went on drinking and talking; a few danced in the bigger room.

Oh, Max. He's at it again. Someone else filled my glass yet again, and to my surprise, it was the young man from the poetry workshop. Nice to see you here. I still haven't forgotten your poem, he told me. And that's a beautiful dress.

We watched the artist for a few minutes, then sat on the wide stairway and talked. He knew a lot about poetry, it seemed. He kept asking if I'd read Robert Bly or Merwin or Seamus Heaney, and I had to keep saying, No.

He was Czech (which explained his accent), his name was Jan, his family had left during the Prague Spring, and his father—a physician in Czechoslovakia—worked as a lab assistant at the university. The party swirled around us as we talked. He'd taken a bottle of wine from the long table in the big room beyond the French doors and kept it on the stairs, pausing now and then to refill our glasses. He told me that the Three Graces had already published books of their poetry; one of them was quite famous.

The poet visited us on the stairs. He drank Irish whiskey from a large tumbler and drops of it sprayed when he laughed, frequently. He had the most amazing laugh. I'd never known poets before—how could I, in my household, my father a radar technician and my mother someone who believed in the sanctity of cleanliness? But they seemed interested in me, these two, and when I mentioned my grandmother and her quilt, Jan's eyes lit up.

He walked me home that evening, and came in to see the quilt. I took it off my bed, into the small living room, and over cups of Earl Grey tea, we looked at each square. I showed him the work I'd done, the new binding sewn over the old, and I showed him how the tiny veins of the leaves in faded gold thread led to brighter gold in protected areas. He told me the names of the leaves in Czech—dubová, the oak; lipa, the linden (though we have a familiar, an affectionate, name for it too, he said; we call it lipky); buková, the beech; and javorovy, the maple. He looked thoughtfully at the squares, the patterns of the leaves within them, and the grey sashing—not straight, as one would expect, but meandering at times, so that the block it led to might have an oblong of linen patched between the leaves and the sashing.

Do you know something? It was not posed as a question but as a discovery. I think this quilt is a map.

1969

On one of our camping trips, in late May (my parents took me out of school early so we could take advantage of some extra time off my father had arranged at his job), my father drove off the TransCanada Highway between Lytton and Spences Bridge along a forestry road that led to a beautiful valley of meadows soft with wild flowers and fragrant trees—Ponderosa pine and fir, mostly, and I remember they smelled more intense than they did anywhere else I've been. We parked the trailer in a rough camping area, leaving my mother behind to settle in before making dinner, while we drove on to a creek my father said he'd always wanted to fish. I wandered away to explore while he tinkered with his tackle box and planned his cast.

I saw two women on a sunlit slope, gathering something. I didn't want to bother them, but one waved, indicating I should come closer. She had a basket and a small trowel, and her companion had the same. She showed me the tiny bulbs she had lifted from the ground. Mountain potatoes, she said with a smile. Delicious! And the other woman cut off the leaves of a plant—not every leaf, and I could see blossoms coming on most of the plants—and placed them carefully in her basket. Greens for dinner, she said. Take some! She handed me a small bunch, tied together with stems.

I sat with them for a while, the wind warm on my face, scented with sage, the sight of snow-capped peaks in the distance. A coyote came to the edge of the meadow, perhaps a quarter mile away, and sat watching us. The women talked softly amongst themselves. Eventually I said goodbye and retraced my steps to the creek where my father was taking his rod apart, four sizable trout glistening on the grass beside the car. As we drove down the mountain, we passed many groups of women with children, all of them carrying baskets filled with roots and greens.

When we got back to the campsite, my mother was deep in conversation with a Native woman who'd been walking down the valley. My mother had just purchased a basket the women had offered for sale, a beautiful thing made of coiled spruce root decorated with a pattern of cherry bark and dyed grass that formed a pattern of arrowheads. I joined them and drank tea with them while my father cleaned his fish and got ready to dredge them in cornmeal.

We didn't expect to see so many people, my father said. On the map there's nothing, beyond the streams, the elevations, the distance to the forestry campsite.

My father called it Botanie, pronouncing it like the science of plants, because that's how it looked on the map, but the woman said, No, no, we say Boothawny (she stressed the middle syllable), it means Blanket of Flowers or Blanket of Clouds—depends on who you believe, and she laughed a little. It's where people gather every year and have since the beginning of time to collect food plants and to hunt. Every year, she said, spring, summer, fall. The land always has something for us. And it's good to be together here, good to remember how our parents came, and their parents.

So I knew, even then, that people gathered together in areas, to remember. And that maps had the capacity to hold secrets.

I ASKED MY FATHER once if he'd ever tried to learn about his mother's parents. For once, he didn't get cross with me for being nosey. Yes, he said, I tried. I went to the library and looked at city directories, searching for Calderas. I called as many as I could find phone numbers for. But nothing. My mother said it was pointless.

They disappear, they know how, you don't understand, she told me. It's not a little argument that people make up after. I am nothing to them. Therefore, you are nothing.

And then he said, so gently he surprised me, Please don't ask me about this again.

1973

AFTER I LEFT Chora Skafion, I spent a month in Italy, taking a ferry to Ischia, exploring Siena, then Florence, and finally wandering the streets of Rome where I paid for a room for two weeks near the train station and drank my espresso each morning in a tiny bar. My heart was still bruised but more itself. I walked and walked, my footsteps on cobblestones my own, but also inflected by the history of place, by what had happened in these places. In the Piazza del Campo in Siena, postcards showed horses circling the Piazza in the Palio of Siena horse race, depicted in all its colours on the cards, though when I stood on the Piazza's perimeter, I saw only waiters summoning tourists with a white towel to Sit, sit, Signora! If I closed my eyes, I could almost hear the sound of hooves in the warm air, feel the drum of them in my spine. Anyone ever there would have known this. On the Spanish

Steps, I read a little book about Keats and looked at his house, imagining him in the window, coughing, his thin body cleansed of its poems. Then I bought a train ticket to Paris.

Every book I'd read about Paris praised its river, its churches, the arrondissements curled like a snail. I found a room in the 6th, near the Sorbonne, with a hotplate and a windowsill wide enough to hold some perishables in a wooden box the concierge provided. In a kitchen shop near Les Halles, I found a little espresso pot and a faience jug to hold flowers. I decided these would be my constants. Strong coffee and beauty.

The bed had a definite trough in the centre. Finding a way to sleep so that I didn't end up at a cramped angle between the springs required artfulness. And learning to sleep through the church bells that sounded not only the hours but the halves and the quarters took some effort, though what did it matter if I woke in the night? I could always sleep later the next morning. And bells filled the night with such beautiful music! I shopped on the Rue Mouffetarde for a slice of cheese, a fresh baguette, a few apples and a bottle of wine; I loved stopping for a paper cone of roasted chestnuts. And if I was careful with my money, I could afford a concert each week in one of the churches on my side of the river—Saint-Séverin, Saint-Julien-le-Pauvre and, once, a transcendent cello performance of Bach in the jewelled glass box that was Sainte-Chapelle.

Strolling along the river one day, towards the Trocadero, I heard a zurna. Maybe two, and a drum. A dauli? My heart stopped. A zurna in Paris? I'd seen the Roma musicians by the Metro or in squares or public markets. Accordians, fiddles, guitars and sometimes a pair of young girls dancing—the music lured me, kept me standing in the rain, listening. I *knew* it somehow. But I hadn't heard a zurna outside of Greece—once in Athens, after I'd left Crete and was wondering the best way to get to Italy. Its wail moved me, prolonged and eerie; and I loved its low hum, like a crooning rising out of the earth. So that day, in Paris, almost afraid of what I'd find, I walked towards the music.

I didn't really expect Nestor, and it wasn't. The protos was an older man, with a generous belly, and the drone player looked like he might be his son. The dauldzis was tall and thin, and nearly bald, his face serious as he slowly tapped with his left hand then suddenly gave a big thump with the beater in his right hand. The music caught me and carried me along with it, and I followed the small procession of musicians and wedding guests as they turned on the Rue Georges Bizet, where a Greek church waited to welcome them. I watched the wedding party enter the tall doors. The musicians put their instruments down outside the church and took out cigarettes. One of them, the dauli player, saw me and beckoned me to join them.

He tried some Romani, but I could only mumble the one or two words I knew. He laughed and made a joke to the others. Then Greek. The same. He laughed again and asked, in French, what language I *could* speak, and I told him, in English, Almost nothing but English, though a tiny bit of French from school. I was making a fool of myself but I couldn't help it. The protos offered me a cigarette. No, but thank you. I heard the zurnas, I said, and couldn't help but follow. I knew a zurna player on Crete . . .

Nestor Bantinakis?

Yes, I said, surprised that they knew immediately whom I meant.

He gets around, that one. Girls at his feet, drawn to the horn. When he said that, the other men laughed. Another man said, enviously, All that time in New York and now Australia for a big-time gig. His wife didn't want to go, she never does, but he convinced her somehow. The kids, eh. She didn't want to take them from school.

I felt heavy and clumsy, in my jeans and brown sweater. So now I knew, but what had I expected? For him to chase me from one end of the Earth to the other? Or even to pick up my trail across Crete? I told Nestor when I met him that I had no idea how to seduce a man and I meant it, but I also had no idea about men in general: how their minds worked, how their bodies worked (though I learned more than I'd have thought possible in my weeks with Nestor) nor how to keep one once I had him in my bed and heart. Or how to recognize a man who might be married to someone else. Who might have slept with any girl in the town, if not me.

Who was a father.

1974–77

THOSE YEARS AFTER my father died, my mother visited my grandmother faithfully. Her own parents were dead—her mother, of cancer, when my mother was still in her teens; and her father, in a car crash, just after she'd married my father. She still drove to Edmonton each summer, though no longer pulling the trailer, which she had sold. Several times I drove with her, when I was between jobs. It felt strange to travel those highways, the same roads we'd taken each summer as a family: the Trans-Canada to Kamloops, then Highway 5 to Tête Jaune Cache, picking up the Yellowhead to Edmonton. Strange to pass the campsites where we'd stayed for one or two nights so my father could fish: Skihist, just north of Lytton, Juniper Beach by Savona, a beautiful site on the North Thompson by the turn-off to Wells Gray Park and, best of all, the places along the Fraser River just as it left its headwaters, a dripping spring by Fraser Pass near Mount Robson, where the pools stood deep blue and azure, nothing like the muddy muscularity of it near Hope. My mother and I stayed at motels on lonely stretches of the highway where we felt our dollars meant something to the owners, small units, with radiators that rattled and shower curtains that had seen better days. We'd arrive at my grandmother's full of these things, full of water, the changing trees of the Yellowhead, firs and pines to larches and black spruce, views of mountains from motel windows hung with yellowing curtains and, most of all, the absence of my father. The empty seat in the car as we parked by my grandmother's house, the empty space at her table. Again.

1978

THERE ARE VILLAGES, he said, in the Beskydy Mountains, surrounded by forests of these trees. My parents took us there on walking holidays. We often stayed in a guesthouse and walked in the Mionsi Forest or through the river valleys. You'd swear some of the narrow roads had never seen a car, and we saw wagons even then, and sometimes gypsies. Or do you say Roma? I don't want to be offensive.

I don't really know. When I was growing up, everyone said "gypsies," though not my grandmother. And then I noticed a shift to Roma. I once knew a Roma man in Greece who told me that "Yifte" was a terrible thing for a non-Roma person to call a Roma. So I can't say what's correct or not. But you'd see them, with wagons?

Yes. And I remember how we loved to stop and touch the horses. In rain, they smelled so pungent, and we'd carry that smell on our hands all day! My mother once bought a ring from a very old woman, and after she'd worn it for an hour or two, it turned her finger green. My father asked, What did you expect, for a few korunas? So we'd walk, and sometimes we'd camp, though my mother didn't like to sleep in tents. If you knew someone, you could arrange to stay in one of the cabins found up in the high parts of the forest, and occasionally we stayed in one for a few nights. I remember waking in the fog one morning in a cabin by a clearing. I remember how the trees looked right then, like huge animals at the edges of the darkness where no light could penetrate the forests. You could hear music far off, fiddles, accordion: probably the family we'd met in the wagon the day before. A photographer in Prague loved those mountains and photographed the trees. My father knew him a little. We have a catalogue from one of his shows. I'll bring it so you can see what I mean.

He looked so animated, remembering, and I could almost see the forests he described, with the winding roads between them, the villages appearing for a moment, then the road again, leading away, curving along a river or skirting the trunk of an ancient maple. And I felt that they were part of me, part of who I was, without my ever having known this. That a grove of beech trees might have sheltered members of my family, people who moved in wagons across great distances, the horses blowing and steaming in rain, and children running alongside, begging for sweets in the villages along the way.

I was thinking this, lost in a kind of nostalgia for something I'd never known but that hid in my DNA, a tangle of roots and tendrils under a dense covering of leaves, when Jan reached out and took my hand. I think you should go.

Go? You mean to Czechoslovakia? Isn't it impossible to get in? My heart sped up as though I already approached its border. I had a little money saved, and there was a modest sum from the sale of my grandmother's house, to be used for something special, something important. My mother said she would let me decide when and what that might be. And even as I said the word *impossible,* I knew he was right.

He made a noise with his lips. Pssht. And flicked his fingers in the air. Not impossible. Not for you. I couldn't return. But you, well, you'd need a visa. It would take some time. And officially it's not permitted to simply wander around the country on your own, but I know people who could help you.

He sipped his tea and then asked, Do you have any more poems?

I did have one. I read it to him in candlelight.

In its eyes, the courtyard outside
        the taverna in Chania, in its eyes
the oblong of bed looking out to Faros. Bees in the celandine, the
red poppies,
prickly gorse, daisies holding the sun to their centres as I
held him
to my breasts. I reach my hand
to the goat and hear bells, the faint sound
        of Nestor rubbing my body with oil,
the rough pumice of his hands.

Jan sighed, and ruffled my hair.

I walked with him until well after midnight, down Oak Bay Avenue and then Fort Street, as far as Cook Street. We encountered a few cars, a bus, a police car slowing as it passed us, wondering if we were drunks. At Cook Street, we said goodnight. He shook my hand, formally, then continued on his way to his family's home in James Bay, and I walked back to my apartment, planning how I'd get to Czechoslovakia.

1974

SHE ALMOST NEVER spoke of my grandfather. I knew he'd built the house in Beverly, with help from a young man he'd hired. It was a modest house. But near the river and near a Catholic church, which my grandfather attended. And not far from my father's school, where my grandmother accompanied him in order to learn to read and write.

He came from a small town near Ostrava. His father had been a miner—and died early for his efforts. This much I knew from my father, who would grow maudlin if he drank and lamented his own father's death before he had much of a chance to know him. But I learned few details about who my grandfather might have been. A saint, as far as my father was concerned. But privately my mother told me that was only because he hardly knew him. Oh, he was no doubt a good man, she granted, but almost certainly not a saint. It made me wonder what my grandmother had told her.

My grandmother burned a candle on his name day—October 4th František from birth, he became Frank in Canada. We had one photograph of him, stern and dark-eyed. I tried to see the young man who had bewitched my grandmother in steerage aboard the *Mount Temple* and had led her away from her family in New Brunswick. I tried to see them as they were then, young—she might have been seventeen or eighteen; the Roma didn't often record the births of their children, wary of officialdom in all its forms. Modesty required her to wear a headscarf. And her gold hoops, coins sewn into her braids. Was she beautiful? I studied her face and couldn't decide, couldn't see the girl hidden in an old woman's features. Eyes so dark as to appear black; a nose not pretty but perhaps strong. She wore so many layers, none of them form-fitting, that I couldn't tell if she was sturdy or lumpy. Two people, kissing behind a lifeboat, while the ship moved inexorably towards a new country, a new life for all its passengers, in steerage or first class, in sickness and in health.

1978

WHEN I WOKE the morning after the party, I went to the kitchen to make coffee and saw the teacups from the night before still on the trunk I used as a coffee table. A cushion from the wooden chair lay tipped into the basket from Botanie, which my mother brought one day to my apartment, saying it would suit my place better than it suited hers. A jolt, a reminder—Jan impatiently pulling the cushion from behind his back and tossing it aside as he talked. A friend, I thought. I have a friend. I took the cup that Jan had used for his tea and touched the rim where his mouth had been. I intuited that Jan was probably gay or at least ambivalent about sex. There had been no frisson in the hours we spent together talking at the poet's party and then in my small apartment afterwards. But how wonderful to have someone to discuss things with—poetry (though he knew so much more than I did), travel, the code he felt was stitched into my quilt.

I'd become resigned to my loneliness. It wasn't debilitating. I did on my own what most people did in couples or groups. I went to the occasional movie, I rode my bike to Dallas Road and then walked around Clover Point, exhilarated by the feel of salt wind on my face. I ate a meal with my mother every few weeks but always with the sense that I had disappointed her. In her widowhood, she had in some ways become more liberated than she'd been as the wife of a gloomy and weak Slavic husband. She had a cheerful social life with other women in her Cook Street neighbourhood. They lawn-bowled in summer; made meals for the elderly in winter, aprons pulled firmly over their sweater sets and polyester trousers; took bus trips to Reno and Disneyland; and played bridge religiously on Friday nights, taking turns in each other's homes with the hostess providing a late-night lunch of crustless sandwiches and various squares, though I had to hope my mother didn't use her dense homemade bread for these. How many of the ladies knew my mother's mother-in-law was a gypsy, I wondered. No matter. She was busy with her friends, and I don't know how she explained me to them. She might never have been the woman with the golden legs on a riverbank, ready to pump up the stove in the trailer. I know she wished for a daughter who did something clean and uncomplicated. Worked in a bank, taught primary school, typed for a lawyer. (A second-hand bookstore?) And had a boyfriend, or by now a husband, and children for whom my mother could knit—sweaters patterned with ducks or kittens, mittens with colourful strings.

When I told her I'd been invited to a party, I knew she imagined a bright room with punch and inventive canapés straight from the pages of *Family Circle*, women in cocktail dresses and high heels, men in leisure suits. She hoped for that kind of occasion, for me as well as for herself. Who's having the party, she'd asked, and when I told her, her smile faded. Oh, the one who's on the radio each Halloween, talking about witchcraft, she said, who wears the pentangles and that bushy beard. But she didn't need to make that comment about the poet. The whole city knew who he was.

But—a friend! I had a theory that people developed the skills for friendship at an early age. The years I avoided skipping, avoided the girls in their go-go boots because I wore sensible shoes, the years I read Jane Austen instead of Nancy Drew: that was when I should have been learning friendship. And when my peers attended university... well, no one actually told me it was possible. My parents didn't know. So I went to Europe on my own for a different kind of education. Alone, and accustomed to my own company.

And now someone showed up at work to invite me for coffee, who asked if he could read any recent poems I'd written, who suggested I join him in one of his favourite activities, which was to take the bus to the end of the line, explore for an hour and then take the bus back to the city's centre. And who took me shopping to the Goodwill at the foot of Yates Street where he found a black velvet dress for me, a small sequined hat with a veil. A pair of grey flannel men's trousers with a cuff and tabs inside the waistband for suspenders. And for himself, a pair of riding boots from some deceased major, the inner label indicating provenance on Jermyn Street. All of these things cost less than a pair of socks at one of the city's department stores.

1973

I DISCOVERED THE JARDIN des Plantes in Paris and walked there most mornings. By late June, the bulbs were finished and the roses beautifully blooming. Lavender, sweet herbs, the babble of children heading in parades over to the zoo—I'd sit on a bench in sunlight and watch, inhale, make notes, which were losing the edgy sting of lost love. Students from the botany programme made their rounds of the gardens, memorizing species and shape. Gardeners kept beds free of weeds and visitors from the grass. Some days I simply sat on a bench, and other days I paid the fee to enter the alpine garden and visit the ancient cedar, which reminded me of home. The fronds filtered light, their shadows on the path like a map of the world. Picking up a fallen branch quickly, so the gardener who'd scolded me for overstepping the path to read a label on a grey-leaved herb wouldn't see, I crushed the bitter green in my left hand. It was incense, it was memory. If I breathed in deeply, I could find my way home.

I drew the plants, not well, with a view to using my eyes to examine them objectively. The petals and stems, the perfection of an anther—I wanted to have them in my notebook so they'd be available to me forever. How a rose opened on a warm morning, from bud to full flower, a poppy bursting from its rough sepals. The succulence of purslane, the delicate habits of violets.

I walked back along the river to my room, pausing to watch the ducks and the lovers. Once I took myself to Berthillion on Île Saint-Louis and ordered a coupe of something rich and creamy, flavoured with prunes soaked in Armagnac. It cost more than I usually spent on food for three days, so I ate bread for the next three days and was glad to remember that ice cream, the mounds of it in a chilled metal dish, beaded with water, whenever I thought I was hungry. It sustained me beyond its mere caloric value.

1978

THERE ARE VILLAGES, *he said, in the Beskydy Mountains, surrounded by forests of these trees.* I wrote this into my notebook. Elements in the quilt still puzzled me. The patches of black velvet, now rusty with age. And some of the stitching in yellow thread, fine as bird tracks. I pondered, and repaired. I finished the binding, the frayed edges of loden wool tucked under as neatly as I could manage. The quilt still smelled smoky, but it was the smoke of ages. I said that aloud—the smoke of ages—and heard how melodramatic it sounded and laughed at myself for it. But the smell did not go away, an elusive blend. Cottonwood smoke from the

North Saskatchewan River, ancient tobacco from my grandfather's handrolleds (my grandmother never smoked, but she'd kept the tins from his Player's tobacco; they held twists of paper with seeds inside, rusted bolts, small coils of wire, the head of a hammer), beech and oak and maple and linden from the forests of the Beskydy Mountains. When I made my bed in the morning, I smoothed out my grandmother's gift, her mother's gift. *Cresses green culled beneath a stone,/And given to a woman in secret.*

But wait, I said aloud. Those stitches, fine as bird tracks... Maybe they *were* birdtracks, maybe they were a trail, a *patrin*. I looked more closely. One set of faded yellow tracks led into beech leaves, then disappeared. Another followed the edge of a winding length of sashing and then circled on itself.

After phone calls to various consular offices, I sent my passport to Montreal for a visa so I could enter Czechoslovakia. Jan advised me to begin in Prague. He had friends who would help me. Some things I should remember and not write down. A few addresses. Names. The location of an apartment where writers got together to produce samizdat, though that might change, and if no one answered my knock, I wasn't to leave a note on the door or talk to neighbours. I might be followed but he'd advise me on clothing so I wouldn't stand out as a foreigner. Though of course the minute I opened my mouth, everyone would know.

My mother thought I should have the quilt cleaned. She said she doubted it had ever been washed and probably seldom even aired. Chickens entered my grandmother's house, and as for my great-grandmother, well, they had no house. They had a wagon and they camped. I listened to her, smiled, nodded and privately determined that my quilt would never undergo such a cleansing. It held all I owned of that side of my family—its smoke, its secret map, the weight of a Roma woman's hands in the early 20th century, the steam of her cooking pot, and the remnants of a cloak, a mattress, a worn blanket at its heart.

1973

WHEN I LEFT Paris for England, I knew I could either stay for a brief time, living on the last of my savings, or I could try to find temporary work—perhaps as a barmaid or a cleaner. An American girl I met on the boat train told me these jobs were usually available on a cash-only basis, without a work permit. I could also try charities, she said. Bernardos, the Cheshire Homes, others. She had a few addresses, which I wrote into my notebook, along with the address of a cheap hostel in Holland Park, a nice neighbourhood she said, though the hostel was a bit of a dump. I found my way there and took a bunk in a room with seven other girls. I also located a charitable foundation and went for an interview. They offered me a position at a halfway house for ex-psychiatric patients in Wimbledon, which included a room, food and five pounds a week pocket money. I cashed my second-to-last traveller's cheque and paid for a Mainline ticket to Wimbledon, settling in the front room of one of two buildings that housed residents ranging from former alcoholics and schizophrenics to men who had served time for murder but who had endured leucotomies or lobotomies and now worked as street sweepers, sharing a room with four or five others in the shabby Victorian houses at the heart of the Foundation's work. The small scar on the forehead of one man made me shiver, but my coworkers assured me he was harmless. Now.

Most days I filled in for cleaners, who quit regularly because they were paid so little, or for the cook, who was Italian and temperamental. With only a modest budget, at any one time she might have 25 people to cook for. That meant big pans of macaroni and cheese, tinned fruit with custard for dessert. Or spaghetti with bolognaise sauce, despite the resulting complaints about foreign food. I made cakes with self-rising flour and currants to go with the fruit and custard and put plates of leftover cake on the table in the TV room later in the evening. This made me popular with some of the residents, and soon a few were inviting me to the pub in the evenings. Usually the cook was coaxed back to work after a few days, and I'd accompany young residents to job interviews or help the nurse to measure and distribute medication. Or I'd return to mopping bathroom floors and taking out garbage.

On my days off, I walked up to Wimbledon Common, stopping on the way to buy a little bag of Callard & Bowser liquorice toffees in a shop with mullioned windows and a whole wall lined with jars of sweets. Often I had to wait while small children crowded the counter with their pennies and shillings, asking for tubes of sour sherbet, sugar mice and unnaturally coloured lollipops. I spent the afternoon on the Common, walking trails, or watching dogs chase balls across the vast expanses of grass, and lovers kissing under spreading trees. Some days were cold—by now it was November—and I'd find a bench, sit on my hands to keep them warm and eat my toffees. On my way back to the Home, I usually visited the horses in a stable partway up the Downs, where I stroked their necks and pressed my cheek to their soft faces. Often there'd be a crisis to face when I returned. Someone hadn't been taking a medication, a recovering alcoholic had relapsed and had to be collected from the train station or the cook had quit again with a complaint that all her self-rising flour had disappeared.

I read voraciously. From a bookshelf in the television room, I took several books at a time to read in my room. Edith Hamilton's *Mythology* entranced me for in it I found stories of Greece. All those gods and goddesses and the heroes and their long voyages, wearing wreaths of laurel or else draped in leopard skins, carrying elaborate shields. And then another book, a dictionary of mythology, which I read like a novel, stopping in my mental tracks when I came to Pan. "Pan was a herdsman's god and inevitably came to be seen as part goat. He loved the wild country and the mountains, and was a notable musician with the syrinx or pan-pipes of seven reeds . . . what was remarkable about him in the context of Greek religion was his total detachment from any social or moral value. He *was*, he had always been, and perhaps even more than any deity in Greek imagination, personified instinct." Whom did I recognize in these words but Nestor, though his zurna had two reeds, not seven? But his grace and appetites were the goat's—how he turned me in the bed, nibbling my ear, pushing at my back with his nose, his cock. His instinct was to make love to women, and I was numbered among them. Special, dressed in new boots and a blue gown, but not permanent.

There was a night watchman, David Hedley, whom I only met on my last day at the Home. But every morning, when I went to the office to learn my assignment for the day, I'd read his entries in the Night Book, scribed in ornate, beautiful handwriting. A former resident, he had so impressed the staff that they'd hired him to patrol the houses each night, to make notes on arrivals and departures, and on any significant events. He had the authority to call the warden if he thought it necessary. He wrote about me in his Night Book—that he'd seen me returning from a late-night walk, that he heard me humming in my room, that I cleaned the bathrooms so much more efficiently than the official cleaners. Sometimes his notes were strangely lyrical—he said I looked like a young Yvonne de Carlo, sultry, dark-haired, dark-eyed. My secret admirer, the staff joked. I heard him, too, patrolling the halls at night, the creak of the stairs under his feet.

1978

AS I SEWED the last few inches of new binding onto the quilt, I heard a faint rustle under my needle. I worked my finger into the small opening and felt something, paper I thought, so I carefully unpicked enough of my stitching to allow its removal.

And it was paper. A tiny scrap in the palm of my hand, so brittle I thought it might turn to dust if I blew on it. The faint printing on it consisted of only eight words, in a script and language foreign to me. I'd already found stems of ancient grass in the batting, a tiny black feather, and even a few long strands of hair, the kinds of things that cling to blankets, particularly ones that might have been used outside, or aired out over fences. I'd put them into an envelope, and I placed the scrap of paper with them. Then I finished sewing the binding to the quilt.

What was I looking for, in the texture of the quilt, in my plan to travel to Czechoslovakia? Not family was it? For some of them surely lived in Canada or North America, and even though my father said he'd tried to find them, I hadn't yet tried—and maybe I'd have more success. No, I looked for something else, hard to express in language, but perhaps where I had originated, the part of me that slept under the quilt's weight at night, the part of me that had listened to my grandmother mutter to herself in the kitchen, who drank her bitter teas, held out my arms for the foul-smelling balm she rubbed into mosquito bites.

And maybe I was looking for my grandmother's childhood, how I imagined her as a girl among sisters and brothers, lithe and carefree, with her whole life ahead of her.

1978

I DREAMED OF MY grandmother singing to her bees. I listened, trying to hear the words. They weren't English, but somehow I understood.

> Peren prajta, peren,
> ča man na učharen.
> Ča man na učharen
> šargona čikaha.
> Sar man učharena,
> o čhave rovena,
> gav gavestar phirna,
> la da orovena.

She sang about being covered with leaves, not only yellow earth, and about children crying, looking for their mother. She sang another song, and this one I heard in English:

Small woods,
cemetery in their midst.
My mother is sitting there.
All crying for her, God,
small woods crying, God.
My mother's crying, God, dear God, crying.

And as she sang, the bees entered the darkness of their skeps. Winter had arrived.

1979

I COULD FLY CHEAPEST to Frankfurt, on late winter fares, and take the train to Prague. An indirect route, the train went in one direction, and then another, overnight, screeching to a stop at stations in the dark. Peering out the small window, I'd see a sign saying Berlin or Dresden. I lost track of where we were, dozing in the shabby carriage in a stale grey cloud because it seemed every German chain-smoked. I tried moving to another seat, but nothing changed. So I dozed, using my extra sweater as a pillow, and dreamed of fresh air, waking to drink strong coffee from a plastic cup, to eat a ham sandwich bought from a man pushing a trolley down the narrow aisle.

At the border, the train stopped. Men with guns and stern looks took our passports into the aisle to peer at the photos, and over at us, conferring in low voices as they examined them. I saw mine being thumbed through carefully, the page with the visa studied for what seemed like an eternity. I hoped they wouldn't demand to search my suitcase—Bring a suitcase, Jan advised, not a rucksack, so they won't assume you're a hippie. I had stashed my notes and little drawings of the quilt, along with Jan's whimsical memory-maps of the Mionsi Forest, in the zippered compartment, and I was paranoid enough to imagine that they'd think I was a spy. Or worse.

But the official who took my passport handed it back to me and said something in a low guttural voice. I didn't understand him and whispered, Pardon me?—my voice breaking in terror. He smiled. Welcome to Czechoslovakia.

My excitement rose as we approached Prague, though the countryside was so lovely in places that part of me longed to disembark and walk away into the hills with their eloquent leafless trees. Patches of snow on the ground reminded me that it was winter, though at home snowdrops and crocuses bloomed. Through the window, remnants of haystacks here and there, dark smoke over small cities, hawks over the fields, stations with uniformed men waiting to help passengers climb down the steps.

Before I left Canada, Jan gave me careful instructions: Wait until the train stopped at Hlavni Nadrazi, the main station in Prague. Get off, go to the main entrance and wait there. I did. Everything was grey and dirty. Train stations smell entirely of travel, gusts of dusty wind as the engines pull in or out, old smoke, the sweat of those emerging bleary-eyed from the carriages. People rushed past me for trams or one of the derelict taxis waiting in front of the station. I tried to look inconspicuous but stood off to one side and waited. Someone touched my elbow.

Patrin. I'm Tomas. Let me take your case. We go this way. Before I could object, he'd grabbed my suitcase and walked quickly away from the station. I walked just as quickly, a little bewildered after the long and virtually sleepless journey from Canada to Prague. From behind, he was stocky, dark-haired.

We turned onto a narrow cobbled street and again into an even narrower alley. We won't go in the front door, he said. The concierge reports every visitor. I saw no lights apart from a searchlight beaming across the rooftops. Tomas unlocked a door, and we climbed steep stairs. Another door.

Here. It's home. He made a grand gesture with his hands and laughed. We had entered a room with a sink and the tiniest stove imaginable at one end, a bed against the opposite wall, a table by the window. Tomas snapped on a goose-necked lamp that emitted a warm yellow glow and illuminated posters on the walls. He put my suitcase near the bed and produced two glasses and a bottle. Pouring a measure into each glass, he looked me in the eyes and said, Na zdravi! Welcome to Czechoslovakia!

He tossed his back. I sipped. Something bitter and herbal. What is it, I asked. It tastes like Christmas.

Tomas laughed. Becherovka. Uniquely Czech. Just don't get drunk on it, or you'll never forget, nor want it ever again, which would be sad, because it's medicinal. Now, you will have the bed. I've put on clean sheets. Toilet is out the door and down the hall.

First right. Shared with others. If the door's closed, knock. If you are sleepy, you can go right to bed. But if you like, we can talk about plans.

I felt sleepy, of course, but too excited to go directly to bed. So we talked. Tomas would be my guide into the Beskydy Mountains. He knew the area well because his parents hiked there (Always the hiking, he said dramatically, rolling his eyes) and his father, before signing Charter 77 (he wrote this down, rather than saying it out loud), had been a professor of graphic arts at Charles University, specializing in the work of Czech photographers. He had no work now but was called upon to sweep streets.

Your English is so good. In Europe I'm always ashamed that I can't speak anything but my own language. A little French, but not even enough to have a conversation.

No one wants to learn our language, so we must learn theirs. And he laughed.

Tomas could not study at a university. And most occupations were closed to him. I asked few questions but could surmise a fair bit from the way he rolled his eyes or made cryptic comments about the weather or changing tides. If the walls didn't have ears, they were certainly thin. He curled up, fully clothed, on a pad on his floor and soon was snoring. I couldn't sleep for ages. And then I fell into darkness, waking once in a wild panic: where was I, who was I, where was my grandmother's quilt? Then I slept again until I woke to Tomas holding a small cup of coffee at my bedside. Light came in like a promise through the small window. If we get started soon, I can show you so much of my city by nightfall.

1974

FIVE MONTHS I lived in my room in Wimbledon, celebrating Christmas quietly with the residents, some of whom had decked the halls with boughs of ivy and long paper chains, giving small gifts to each other, including me (packets of Scottish shortbread and a bag of the toffees I loved). I cooked the turkey, helped by several of the residents, one of whom insisted on making bread sauce that tasted remarkably like the stuffing another had made: bread, milk, an onion in the centre of the bowl, flavoured powerfully with thyme and sage. A neighbour came by with a platter of mince pies, shortbread and chocolate gingers. I turned away for a minute, and when I went to help myself to a mince pie, nothing remained on the platter but the sprig of holly for decoration. In the new year, I walked the Common on my free days, visited the horses, and cooked and cleaned when the help failed to come to work.

One morning I woke to daffodils in the back garden; the greengrocers had small beautiful lettuces from hothouses in Kent, and I knew, simply, it was time to go home. I went into the City to make my arrangements and had a last visit to the British Museum, where I liked to go to a different gallery each time. This time I went to several of them to say goodbye to favourite objects—a votive owl, a small shoe from ancient China, the lion from Persepolis, and what was called the famous false fresco, *Pond in a Garden*, from the Tomb of Nebamun, c. 1350 BC. I didn't know enough to determine why it was false, but I loved it, with its swimming ducks and fish, surrounded by elegant trees; and I loved the big-eyed owl; and the tiny shoe, which had survived its wearer by so many hundreds of years. Then I wandered across Great Russell Street to look in the shops selling Greek antiquities and excellent reproductions; in one of them I found the little sealstone.

I asked the clerk if I could hold it and she took it out of the glass case, handed it to me. I turned it over in my palm and had to brush tears away with my sleeve as I examined the details. These were the goats who'd come to me on the rocks above Chora Skafion, straggles of thyme in their beards, and there, in their bodies, was the memory of Nestor, my modern Pan with his zurna and his tender hands. How much, I asked, and the woman told me 20 pounds. I'd saved most of my pocket money, apart from what I'd spent on trains and liquorice, so I could be reckless. I bought it. She tucked it into a little velvet bag.

The night watchman David Hedley had written more about my comings and goings. Walking back from the train station that day,

I looked at the tall house with its silent windows and wondered which one hid him, watching. I confess I wondered too what he looked like and was startled on the day I left, at a little farewell party organized by the dining room staff, to be introduced to a small man in a soiled, threadbare jacket, very few teeth, a tell-tale scar on his forehead. He gave me a bouquet of flowers and bowed as I accepted them.

1974

MY FATHER'S DEATH made me cold. I hadn't been any help, not in the days leading up, when I visited the hospital with my mother, the two of us walking the long corridor with its smell of disinfectant and floor-wax. It felt like an intrusion to enter the room where he lay with his tubes and his grey face, his eyes distracted and far gazing. My mother held his hands and rubbed them to warm them. Here, Patrin, you try. In my hands, his felt as heavy as stones. A nurse shaved him but not well. His cheeks were rough with whiskers, his breath sour. I wanted to ask questions about our origins, the ones I tried to ask by the fast rivers while he cast for trout, but he wasn't in any state to ask anything of; his shoulders shook convulsively. I could have done more for him, for my mother, but I felt helpless. And already fatherless.

And remorseful because I couldn't show him the kind of physical affection he'd denied me all my childhood.

I couldn't get warm. In Victoria, accompanying my mother to the various places to declare him officially dead—the newspaper office to place the obituary, the crematorium for his remains, the bank to erase his name from their joint account—I wore his down jacket and woollen stockings. I didn't care how I looked. I forgot to wash my hair until my mother took me to the deep sink in the basement, bent me over it and gently shampooed my head, towelling it after. Then she combed out my hair. It took twenty-five minutes. We barely talked. What was there to say? She was a widow. I had no father. I huddled over the hot-air vent from the basement furnace, trying to stop my arms and legs from trembling with cold.

But in my grandmother's bed, under her quilt, my feet thawed, and I drank one of her leafy teas, bitter with sage. In my mother's house, fresh white sheets hung on the line each week, rain or shine, and on the beds lay duvets she'd bought after reading about their European elegance in an issue of *Chatelaine*. The sheets on my grandmother's bed were not so fresh, but I welcomed their rough comfort, and the weight of two heavy woollen blankets, smelling impossibly of sheep, and the quilt.

Did people know she was a Romani woman? Did her neighbours know from her skin, her ceremonies of candles, the piles of wood by her door and the iron pot on the woodstove, steaming with hares she'd skinned and jointed, thickening the broth with their minced livers? Did anyone hear her sing to her bees? I imagine her neighbour, the one who received her huge copper pot, looking at its surface and wondering at its workmanship. Running his thumb around its rim, the hammered iron of its handle.

And if people knew, did it matter? The neighbourhoods of Edmonton had their secrets—people starved out by Stalin, forsaken by their countrymen, driven from one border to another, selling everything for a piece of paper allowing them passage. Were the Roma any different than the Doukhobors, the Mennonites, the sad remnants of Yiddish shtetls in Poland or Lithuania?

1979

WE TAKE THE train tomorrow, to Frenštát pod Radhoštěm. Many people go there because of Janáček, who was born nearby in Hukvaldy. I have papers for you, but here's the thing, you will have to remember that you are a deaf-mute.

What? I looked at him in surprise—and he was smiling.

You need papers for travel. You don't have them. My cousin does but she's deaf. Her papers say this. So I will be your guide. All you will do is look serene and pretend you can't hear. I do the rest. Very important that no one hears you talk on the train. This way it's ok for us to go anywhere that Czechs would go.

We'd spent the day walking the city. His city. A strange combination of achingly beautiful and grimly melancholic in the extreme. The buildings, grey and sombre, the streets patched, areas crumbling. (The tanks came here. And here.) Scaffolding imprisoned the churches. (Though nothing happens. The scaffolds are all Russian theatre, you know. They put it up to keep people out of the buildings, but then they do nothing to repair them.) No one smiled.

Yet the city remained alive. Musicians came to play concerts—Sarah Vaughn, just that year; Johnny Cash. Tourists walked the streets, as we did, but the absence of picture taking was conspicuous—to me at least, who'd travelled to Rome and Paris, and Athens. (It's not that you can't, Tomas explained. But a Czech would know what could and couldn't be photographed. And somehow tourists are reluctant to sit in offices with smooth officials while their film is removed from their cameras because they photographed a security team searching an old man or poking their guns in a woman's ribs.) I'd not expected so many armed men on street corners or covert reflected glances as I looked at the bare shelves through shop windows.

How is it you can take time away from work to help me? It's much appreciated of course, but I hope you aren't losing income. And he offered a cryptic reply: Perhaps this *is* my work.

We ate in a small smoky bar with tiny windows looking out on the Vlatava. We ordered bowls of Česnečka, a sort of national dish, Tomas said: garlic soup, with little cubes of fried bread floating on top; we ordered huge dumplings with carrot gravy over slices of rich pork, and glasses of beer: drinking it, I thought of the haystacks I'd seen from the train. I was one of only three women in the bar. Single men, hunched over beer and books, occupied most of the tables, the covers of their books hidden by pages of newsprint. It is automatic, said Tomas. We make covers for our books because everyone is a possible informant. No detail is too small to take to an office and be given a few korunas in exchange. We say we hated being occupied during the war, but we allow this. Pah. He spit on the sidewalk, then laughed. I hope no one saw, or I'll be visited in the night by men who will search my room for other signs of insurrection.

Over the Charles Bridge with its sad-faced musicians and grey water moving underneath in a stately way, up the Castle steps to the spires of St. Vitus and the Castle itself, then down again. Along the Nový Svet, the low houses so beautiful. Pointing to one of them, Tomas told me it had been the home of the famous astronomer Tycho Brahe who died of a burst bladder at a dinner party where he was too polite to leave the emperor's side. I was entranced by marionettes in shops in the Mala Strana, and stopped to admire the witches, devils, the princesses and kings. I loved their eyes, their animated faces. In a city where glances were furtive, if not downright hostile, where no one smiled, the wide smiles on the marionettes and the wink of a devil impressed me as strangely human.

I love these, Tomas said, indicating house signs as we strolled up Nerudova—a golden key, three lilies, some carved fiddles and even an improbably green lobster. It would be acceptable to photograph them, he told me, and I happily snapped away. And then he quickly steered me into a narrow street, through a courtyard and up some stairs. He knocked on a blue door, two brief taps, then opened it. We entered a long low room where half a dozen young men bent over a table covered with papers. Two looked up. The others continued what they were doing. Which was collating the latest issue of their samizdat newsletter.

1974

My return to Victoria from London was both exciting and anticlimactic. My parents met me at the little airport near Sidney, my father frail and using a cane, my mother smiling. I wore the same jeans in which I had left Canada, tucked into my Greek boots. I carried gifts in my rucksack—Fair Isle mittens from the Scottish shop in Piccadilly for my mother, a bottle of duty-free Scotch for my father.

I'd had a love affair, which made me feel sophisticated, if still a little heart-sore. And I knew Wimbledon Common the way my former classmates knew the trails of Beaver Lake. I knew the protocols of shopping at a greengrocer's—wait in the queue, bring your own string bag, let the grocer handle the tomatoes, don't attempt to pick them up yourself. (By all means buy the Cox's Orange Pippins, even though they look rough and brown. Their flavour is out of this world.) I felt ready for the next chapter of my life, certain it would not resemble the chapter that had concluded with my departure for Europe the year before. That chapter had been quiet—think English lady novelists rather than Jack Kerouac. Quiet summers of picking strawberries at one of the Saanich Peninsula berry farms for pennies a pound and a stint of cleaning motel rooms on the Gorge. Friday nights spent reading in my bedroom. Working at the campsites, at Butchart Gardens.

I owned a tiny sealstone with two goats in an act of coitus, so moving it made me cry to hold it in my hand. I wanted a life in which such images were natural and possible. I wanted books and music, rough weaving to hang on my walls. And so I answered the ad for the bookstore on Fort Street and presented myself for the interview.

1979

I'VE MADE YOU a copy of a map, whispered Tomas, handing me a small square of folded paper. We were sitting on the grubby seats of a railway carriage heading to Brno where we would change trains for Frenštát pod Radhoštěm. She was born, when, 1895 you said, so Moravia looked something like this.

This is from 1882 but mostly the same. And you think she lived... where?

Well, they had a wagon, and my father thought they lived on the road most of the time. When he was a little boy, she told him once or twice what it was like to sleep in a bunk with all her brothers and sisters around her, the horse snorting outside, and the wheels creaking if it was windy. But her father worked for a landowner—in winter, mostly, and I think his property was near Jablunkov. When he worked there, they had a little house to live in.

I looked at the map, remembering what Jan had said: Do you know something? (It was not posed as a question but as a discovery.) I think this quilt is a map.

What else had he told me? *He told me the names of the leaves in Czech—dubová, the oak; lipa, the linden (though we have a familiar, an affectionate, name for it too, he said; we call it lipky); buková, the beech; and javorovy, the maple. He looked thoughtfully at the squares, the patterns of the leaves within them, and the grey sashing— not straight, as one would expect, but meandering at times, so that the block it led to might have an oblong of linen patched between the leaves and the sashing.*

Tomas, I whispered back, Tomas, are there villages in this part of Moravia named for trees? And tell me why we're whispering? There's no one else in the carriage.

Because you are deaf. You can't talk. Remember? And this is a country where the walls have ears, even the walls of a train compartment. Let me look at the other map I have, the one I brought because we are interested in hiking. The questions we ask about places will be reasonable because we are hiking to them. He kicked out his big boot. See! He'd borrowed boots from a friend, with impressive soles and red laces. But let's see on the map. He ran his finger over its surface, the names foreign to me, but I looked anyway. Staré Hamry, Dobra, hmmm, maybe just here, Dubová. Oak, do you know that tree?

Yes, I whispered, and oak leaves are on the quilt.

Quite close to where we are going. Never mind too much walking. He admired his boots again. There are buses. We will go there from Frenštát pod Radhoštěm and see what there is to see. Once we are off the train, you don't have to be deaf any more. Unless I tell you. Then you will let me handle the talking.

Our plan was a game to him but one he also took seriously. The Czechs were accustomed to cryptic talk, to riddles. After all, it was Jan who recognized the quilt as a map, his mind reading the pattern in a way mine didn't, or couldn't. At first. And if in fact that was true—that the grey sashing meant roads, the blocks of leaves meant groves of trees—maybe we would find out. But in the years since, everything might have changed too much for us to tell. I couldn't imagine whom we might ask.

Tomas went back to looking out the window, and I took the map onto my lap and tried to make sense of it. Dubová—yes, I found it. While running my finger along the river that ran in a thin blue line in a north-south direction through Dubová, I saw another of the tree words that Jan had alerted me to. Velký Buková. Tomas, I whispered, look! What does Velký mean?

It means "big" or "large." So that's Big Beech. And see how the road winds along the river, down into this valley, from Dubová to Velký Buková. I wonder if there's a Buková, a smaller village adjacent to Velký Buková? Maybe it's gone now, lost, or hidden. Because large implies that there's also a small, do you agree? Large in this case is probably not very big. But I think we know where we're going now, Patrin.

And he looked pleased. When the conductor came to our compartment, I sat with a far-off look on my face—I'd been practising—while Tomas handed him our tickets. I heard Tomas say something in Czech, nodding towards where I sat, and the conductor said something just as mysterious in return. The train had entered the mountains.

1974

I FOUND THE APARTMENT on Oak Bay Avenue not long after I acquired the job at the bookstore. I could easily ride my bike to work; I could even walk if I set out with enough time. And buses ran by my door. I didn't want to live with my parents. My father was weak, his heart fading more each day, and it took all my mother's energy to care for him. Their pattern of need and response was tightly constructed; better for me to leave them alone.

I had almost no furniture to move into the apartment. Two grey cedar Adirondack chairs from my parents' backyard for the sitting room. A Greek shepherd's bag I'd brought back from Crete and draped over the back of one of the chairs. A mattress, which my father's friend helped me wrestle into the small bedroom and fit onto the base of an old iron-framed bed my mother let me take from the basement of my parents' home. I bought a pine drop-leaf table and two wooden chairs at a second-hand store two blocks from my building. The owner lent me a dolly to move them home. I kept my clothing in a big basket in the closet and placed my small *batterie de cuisine* in the tiny kitchen. (I'd seen a sign advertising *batterie de cuisine* on the door of a kitchen shop near Les Halles in Paris, and I loved it for its suggestion of battle, hard work, dented pans.) My collection was sparse: two knives, one for bread and the other for carving; three plates; one skillet; a copper saucepan found in a junk store, almost unrecognizable as copper until I thought about the reason for the verdigris; a bigger stock pot; two mugs from a potter on West Saanich Road, one of them with a little ceramic frog on the bottom, so that when I drank coffee or tea, I'd see it sitting there, waiting for me to finish. I had a baking sheet and two whisks. An egg beater and one wooden spoon. I had my faience jug that I kept filled with wildflowers gathered from the vacant lot nearby: dandelions, asters, camomile and flax.

I returned to my little home on the first night, after work, and I made myself an omelette and sat to eat it in one of the cedar chairs, softened with a cushion of pale green corduroy. I rinsed my plate and wiped out the skillet with a piece of paper towel. Then I lay on my bed, on top of my grandmother's quilt. I could smell her house in the wool and remembered how it felt to wake in the night to feel her wide back on the bed beside me. I cried a little as I remembered Nestor and his hands on my face, his voice calling me kardia mou. Would I ever share someone's bed again, not my grandmother's, but a lover who would make plans for us? Would anyone share this bed with me?

Two did, as it turned out. A friend of the owner of the bookstore where I worked took me to dinner one evening and drove me home. He walked me to the door, and then stopped inside for a glass of wine. Which led to a kiss, which led to my bed. He lived in Seattle and never returned, not that I knew.

He was terrified of you, the bookstore owner told me later. He said he'd never met a young woman with such a sense of self-containment.

Was I self-contained? Was that another way to describe loneliness?

Another younger fellow frequented the store, looking for books about the occult. We went for drinks in the little bar in the hotel on Beach Drive, and one thing led to another. But he had ideas about bondage and pain; after listening to him describe what he'd like me to do to him, and what he'd like to do to me on our next date, I asked him to leave. He stopped coming into the bookstore for a time and then resumed his searches of the shelves, acting as though nothing had ever happened. On the street, you wouldn't have known him from Adam.

1979

LOOK, SAID TOMAS, quietly. That's a gypsy settlement. The train slowed as we approached the haze of a big city—Ostrava, Tomas told me. We would transfer there to another train.

I looked. A block of apartments, the dreary grey of damp concrete, with small fires outside and children playing near them. Dogs. Even a horse tethered to a pole. A few men leaning over the engine of a car, the hood propped open with a stick. There was nothing of beauty—no gardens, no window boxes, no tidy paths leading to the building itself. Tomas was troubled, I could tell. How much to tell me, how much to leave out? The State insists on them living in proper houses, or flats, but it gives them the worst ones it can, he said. They don't want to live there. They'd rather move around, follow the work, make their own lives. But they have to stay. And everyone else in the neighbourhood moves out. A small boy poked at a fire with a piece of wood. He wore no pants, though it drizzled with rain. One of the men saw us looking at them through the train window, made a rude gesture, and turned away.

They could have been related to me. I wondered to myself if anything could be worse than not knowing your family, even if one of them looked up at you from the huddle of men bent over the hood of a car, looked up at you across the chasm of time and space, of privilege and want. When I confessed this to Tomas, he explained that this group was almost certainly not related to my grandmother, that most Czech gypsies perished during WWII. They call it the Devouring, he said.

The word caused goosebumps to rise on my arms.

He continued: In Bohemia, there was Lety and here in Moravia, Hodonin. And many were also sent to Auschwitz. Slovakia became a protectorate of the Reich, and the Roma population didn't suffer as much. After the war, the Slovak Romanies gradually settled in the Czech lands, mostly after 1958 when it became forbidden to be a nomad. Police cut the wheels off the gypsy wagons, burned them, and that was that. Children were supposed to go to school, but the schools didn't welcome them. The kids were considered backward, though they might have had all kinds of skills other children didn't have. Language would have been a problem, too. We don't understand their language. They know ours, but we don't think of them as citizens. We don't know one another. They keep to themselves except for begging. And I think Czechs are a bit afraid of them because of everything they—we—don't know but suspect, even if it's wrong. And the State interfered with families, taking children from their parents if the parents didn't follow the rules. Look, it has to be said: the gypsies haven't endeared themselves to the rest of the population, so it's not surprising that there would be bad feelings on either side.

How do average people feel about this, I asked.

It's complicated. Most cultures have their scapegoats, is that the word? The Jews in Germany during the last war. Your native Indians, I've heard that they live in rough conditions, not unlike the gypsies.

I don't think the rest of the population wanted them, ever, I said, and then wondered if I was being rude to my host. But I had become increasingly aware of the injustices—the seedy settlements, the hissing in Prague as a Roma woman and her baby crossed the Charles Bridge, that officials had taken entire families into work camps and let people starve. I've never heard these things about the camps, I said. The concentration camps for Jews, yes, but not Lety or Hodonin. Why don't I know? I was filled with grief for events and people I'd never known.

He looked at his hands, crossed his legs, the big borrowed boots awkward on his feet. Then he recrossed his legs, and tucked his hands under his thighs. I don't think it would have been so bad when your grandmother was a child because the rural parts of the country were mostly poor, many people didn't go to school, and it would have been easier for the gypsies to keep to themselves without people noticing them much. Now there's a lot of discrimination and hostility. Czechs think that the Roma get advantages others don't—housing or work. But you see that apartment block, half its windows broken. No one else would want to live there. Most of the time, there's probably no electricity or running water. As I said, it's complicated. And the work! In Ostrava, it's in the coal mines, and so many people get a problem with the lungs. Or they sweep the streets. It's hard to look at their settlements and think them privileged in any way at all.

I turned from the window. What if my grandmother's immediate family had stayed instead of travelling in steerage to North America? Would any of them have survived? And of those left behind, did any traces remain?

When the conductor came around again, he looked directly at me and asked for my ticket. Luckily I remembered I was deaf and didn't indicate that I'd heard him or knew what he wanted. Tomas handed over our tickets and our identity cards, and I made some signs with my hands, as though in question. He did the same, as though to answer. In truth I felt as helpless as a deaf person. Tomas was my hearing, my speaking. What would I have done without him?

SHE PICKED HER serviceberries and her plums; she dried crab apples to flavour winter hares in the simmering pot. Garlic hung in the room where my father had slept. I don't remember her sewing, but she darned socks, loops of grey wool pulling ravelled edges together, whatever the colour of the sock. Socks thus mended were warm, though they gave off the odour of sheep. If I pressed my ear to the inner wall, on the side of the house where the bees wintered in their skeps, I'd hear them murmuring, murmuring. I could almost forget I was in a cold Canadian city and imagine myself instead into a European fairy tale, in socks heavy with lanolin, under a quilt of leaves, listening to workers feeding their proud queen.

After she died, I had the heavy thought that no one told her bees she was gone. My mother sold the house and what happened to the skeps? I imagined them tossed to the burning pile, their combs melting, the bees homeless, wondering where was the woman who sang to them and grew flowers for them, led them to cottonwoods in bloom on the river where they collected the sticky resin they used to keep mice from their hives. She was too heavy to dance, but there was lightness in her when she worked with her bees.

1979

A FORMER CLASSMATE OF Tomas's mother owned a guesthouse. She had kept a room for us— very spare, but clean; two beds, a sink, a chair and a painted wardrobe with hooks for our clothing. She welcomed us with slivovice.

She will not ask questions, said Tomas after she'd left us to our unpacking. And she will keep quiet about us, too.

I have this piece of paper, I said, and I took the envelope out of my case where it was tucked into my Czech phrasebook for safekeeping. It might be nothing…

… or it might tell us something, finished Tomas, taking the fragile scrap to the window for more light. He squinted to bring the faded letters into focus. His lips moved as he sounded out words to himself, then aloud. I heard Dubová, Buková. Other words I couldn't understand. He turned to me, his face alight.

So, he said, it's very hard to read, it's the old writing, and it's faded, but I think four of the words are places—Dubová, Buková, Lipky, and Malyjavorice. We've seen Dubová and Velký Buková on the map, so we know they exist, or did—sometimes these places fade away over time. Lipky would have something to do with lindens. And Malyjavorice—small maples, maybe. And some of the words might be names. Not really Czech, though. Adamu, this looks like, Fifika, Florica, Tas.

Is there someone we could ask?

I'll talk to Mrs. Horakova.

I curled on my side on one of the beds, sleepy after the long train ride—in which I did nothing but sit. Still, as we rumbled over the face of the country my great-grandparents and their children had left so long ago, I accumulated every mile in my heart, elbows and ankles. In this country, my name was not foreign, no one would say, How's that again? Can you spell it? Or laugh at the notion of three consonants knocking together so hard at the beginning: S, Z, K. Sleepy because I was travelling a long road, a track, and I didn't know where or when I would come to its end. My eiderdown smelled like sweet herbs and the pillow was soft. Sleepy because....

Patrin, Patrin, wake up. Tomas gently pushed at my shoulder. There's a man in this town who is married to a Roma woman. Mrs. Horakova went to his house and asked if he would talk to us. And he's agreed. He even speaks some English.

Almost certainly the four words were names. Chavi was adamant about Florica—"means flower," said her husband, Jiři. Fifika was to do with God, a girl's name. And Adamu, well, something like earth. Of Tas she was most certain. A birds' nest, her husband told us after she spoke rapidly, using her hands to shape a nest in the air. Birds in the sky, her fingers flying. Eggs opened, birds flew in and out of the nest, feeding the hungry mouths, or perched quietly, wings folded neatly to the body.

In difficult fragments of English and Czech—and even Chavi's long passionate exposition in a language Tomas told me was Romani and for a moment reminded me of my grandmother speaking to her bees—I learned that, yes, once Roma families had lived in the Beskydy Mountains, moving from place to place—villages; beech woods where they let their pigs, if they had them, feed on ripened nuts in autumn; hidden rivers where they met up with others of their kumpania to share stories, arrange marriages—as the seasons changed and as work opportunities arose. Then the war, and many Roma died. Were taken, by force, to Hodonin or Lety. Or shipped to Auschwitz. Even Chavi's own mother and father, I learned—though Chavi herself was spared and given to a family in Opava to raise. They tried to find her family after the war and nothing, nothing, until much later when relatives from Slovakia claimed her. But she had gone mute in Opava, wouldn't speak Czech, until she was united with her relatives, and then she felt between two languages. And was between them still, with Jiři and their children. (She dreams in Romani, confided Jiři. She *feels* in Romani.) She took my face between her hands and said something fiercely, lovingly. Jiři told me she hoped that I would find something of my family in the villages they had passed through two lifetimes earlier. Your name, he said, translating, is your best prayer.

1978

After Jan came into my life as a friend, after we'd spent time travelling the buses to the end of their routes and exploring the Goodwill, I began to think more seriously about the craft of poetry. I wrote always—but was it truly poetry? I could move words around on the page, group them into lines that resembled poetry. But did I have the right to call it poetry? Some days at work, I'd check the shelves for a book to help me with this, and yes, I found books about the making of poems, but somehow I couldn't follow those instructions. I would have to learn on my own, though I doubted I *could* learn. I remembered those students with their vocabularies, their confidence, their ability to ask questions for which I had no answers.

I'd look at the scribbling in my notebook and try to settle their syllables into the rhythms I heard when I read poems in books. I learned that I could cut a few words and let the lines themselves suggest what the words had said. I could try to make space on the page mimic what I wanted the words to say, to imply.

no one told her bees
    she was gone.
My mother sold the house and what happened
    to the skeps?
I imagined them tossed

to the burning pile, their combs
melting,
the bees homeless,
wondering where
was the woman who sang to them
and grew flowers for them,
led them to cottonwoods
in bloom
on the river where
they collected sticky resin
to keep mice
from their hives.
She was too heavy
to dance
though there was
lightness
as she worked
with her bees.
And those bees,
hovering,
homeless.

When I finished working with this series of notes, I thought it resembled the complicated dance or return of bees to the hives in alcoves set in the walls of my grandmother's house—random, but not; individuals and clusters, their legs heavy with pollen.

I loved trying to make the words move as bees move, as my grandmother moved in her garden, weighted to the ground with her baskets and sticks. Her wagon nearby, filled with cottonwood boughs from the banks of the Saskatchewan River, her dog trembling in the grass.

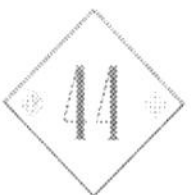

1979

WHAT ARE THOSE? I watched Tomas as he removed papers from his case, and found a place for them inside his jacket.

He held up a copy of the samizdat newsletter so I could see. When we'd arrived at the apartment in the Mala Strana, we'd immediately pitched in to help collate the latest issue. I was introduced and given the job of stapling. The entire issue was in Czech, so I couldn't begin to understand it but could recognize several poems and something that looked like an essay.

As the young men and women worked to bring their newsletter to life, they laughed a lot. Tomas explained that several of the group had just been released from detention and this was a bit of a celebration. That explained the bottles of sekt that made the rounds, poured into whatever glasses or mugs they found. Someone gave me a tin mug, and I drank from it gratefully; we'd been walking for hours, and I was so thirsty. One boy—hardly a man—tipped the last of the wine directly from a bottle into his mouth.

A woman called for quiet by waving her shoe in the air and then read a poem from the page she held close to the light, an extra from the newsletter. I couldn't understand, but she read it so movingly that I found myself hoping for a translation. She saw my face and said, Shall I translate for you? And yes, I said, yes, please.

It's Jan Skácel, she said. One of our great poets. This is a love song. She took some time to write on a scrap of paper, erase, think, erase. I could hear her pencil. Then she looked up again, smiling.

> Don't fear the voices, there's a lot of them,
> the wind has combed the grass
> the past few days,
> someone is making love on the dishevelled straw
> and the plucked autumn's waiting in the maize.
>
> Like a bird behind the hangman, a cloud follows the sun,
> the heavens lie a-bleeding
> and it's beyond my strength.
> The astringent yellow you carry in your hair
> they've scattered from their carts on the rough tracks.

Oh, I thought, then said it aloud: Oh! It's so beautiful. And I knew it was somehow about my family, their journey. I was the cloud, following their sun. The strands of grass, scattered from their carts were caught in the batting of the quilt I restored. The words were part of the story I was in search of.

The young woman—Barbora—and I talked, while the bottles were drained around us and the remains of the sausage and bread devoured. She was fiercely funny and told me of cat-and-mouse chases through the Mala Strana with a Gestetner in her backpack (I just about toppled backwards on the hills, she said) to avoid the security police. But this is the way we share our literature, she said. The pigs give us no option. We won't stop writing and reading our banned writers just because they tell us we can't. But you must forget you were ever in this room. The room isn't important anyway. There will be somewhere else next month.

So now in the small room at Mrs. Horakova's guesthouse, I asked, What will you do with them? And he said he'd arranged—but how? I hadn't see him talk to anyone—to drop them off with a man who would see that they found their way into the right hands. This is how the new writing, the important ideas, make their rounds, he told me—like leaves in the wind!

May I have a copy for myself, I asked. And he said no, too dangerous—for you but also for me.

I want the poem by Jan Skácel, I told him. Even though I can't understand Czech, I want it.

Then you will have to take it to heart, he said. Is that the right way to say it?

Yes, I replied. Yes, I will take it to heart.

15

OFTEN I DREAMED of Crete. In my loneliest (or most self-contained) moments, I wondered if I'd ever have the experience again of waking to a man making me coffee on a terrace overlooking the sea, water glittering, the geometric shapes of the buildings radiating sunlight. Were geraniums ever that red, the air that exotic—donkeys and bread, the almond scent of oleanders, tang of fish as women carried home the evening's dinner wrapped in damp newspaper? I walked through the old quarter of the city most mornings, exhilarated by hours of solitary exploration because it made the reunion with Nestor after his classes even sweeter. Once I bought figs at the market and brought them back to our room where we fed each other slices of the honeyed pink flesh, washed down with golden wine.

When I walked the streets of my city, stopping for coffee or pausing at windows to admire a display of dresses, I sometimes longed for someone to talk to me about the books I was reading or to hold my face and kiss my eyes. Kiss my mouth. Unbraid my hair as Nestor did in Chania and pull me down to the bed.

Yet dreaming of Crete did not mean that I wanted to return. I couldn't imagine entering the city alone instead of hurtling towards it in the passenger seat of a Deux Chevaux, cradling a velvet bag containing a polished zurna. My heart wouldn't allow me to go there.

1979

MRS. HORAKOVA'S HUSBAND lent us his ramshackle motorcycle. He didn't need it during the day because the school where he taught young children was a short walk from the house, though he stressed that he wanted it back for the evenings when he often rode to a neighbouring village to drink beer with his brother and play cards. Mr. Horak did something mysterious to the spark plug and funnelled petrol into the tank from his stash in the shed, adding oil from a grimy little bottle. He found one helmet in the shed where he kept his chicken feed. Mice had been nesting in it, but he brushed out the little pocket of dried grass and chicken fluff, blew a couple of times to loosen the last turds, then handed it to me with a smile. Děkuji, I said, and he smiled. Prosím.

Have you driven a motorcycle before, I asked Tomas, who was relieved he would not have to hike. Once, he said, as we raced away from Frenštát pod Radhoštěm. Past the small houses with their bitten yards, curtains twitching. Past the last store with its dog tied to the front door. Mrs. Horakova had made lunch for us—her dark bread spread with chopped garlic and fresh cheese curds, some frgál (the delicious pastry we'd had for breakfast; it looked like a pizza but was filled with a dense pear paste sprinkled with ground almonds), and dried plums from her tree—and had put tea in a thermos, adding two slices of precious lemon. Děkuji, děku, I told her. And we had our maps: Tomas's map of this part of Moravia and my sketch of the quilt.

The wide road narrowed a few miles out of town. Narrowed to a tunnel through trees just coming into leaf, though snow remained on the ground, particularly as the road ascended. We were in the Beskydy Mountains, and I smelled spruce.

As we approached the borders of the forest, Tomas pointed to a sign: Malyjavorice. Small maple, he called over his shoulder. A sign with a coat of arms, brightly painted, a maple leaf featured in one quadrant, a hawk in another. But if you blinked for a moment, you missed the village itself. Four houses, a collapsing barn, a shop. Which was open, so we stopped. Tomas went in first, called Dobry den to an ancient woman sitting by a woodstove. A table beside her held an old-fashioned scale, with weights, and a steel cash box: her counter. In the stove, something acrid and smoky burned.

The woman was almost completely blind. Yet she crocheted, a task I'd thought impossible without sight, but her hook never stopped, and the reel of cotton by her side transformed itself little by little into delicate lace. She spoke no English but took my hand in greeting, patting it repeatedly as Tomas explained to her that I'd come from Canada in search of information about my great-grandparents who'd travelled through here in the early years of the century. She listened and muttered something.

She has lived here forever, she says, Tomas told me. And before her, her parents, her grandparents and generations before that, all in Malyjavorice. One uncle was a forester. He worked in the Mionsi.

The room—a store that held several armchairs and the strong-smelling wood stove, a dog on a filthy rug, tiny windows hazy with dust and shelves almost completely bare apart from jars of pickles, sacks of coal, a bucket of onions and a box holding three packets of cigarettes—felt to me as if it held itself intact in history, with old photographs pinned on the walls, faded portraits of dour women, stern men, unsmiling children staring at the camera, a funeral. A broken spinning wheel in one corner spoke of the days when sheep had ruled the Beskydy Mountains (I remembered the smell of lanolin in my grandmother's house), and shadowy filtered light entered through murky windows.

I've told her you are looking for information about your family, said Tomas, and she wants to feel your face.

What?

It's how she reads. It's okay. Let her.

So I leaned towards her, and she let the crocheted lace fall to her lap. Her hands were rough but somehow kind as they shaped my face, her fingers stroking my eyelids and the bridge of my nose, my mouth. Cikán? She phrased it as a question. Tomas said something quietly to her, then to me. A little, yes, her great-grandparents, and her grandmother, all from around here. Her grandfather, from near Ostrava—no, he wasn't gypsy but from miners. That's right, yes? He looked at me and I nodded. I can't tell if she disapproves, he said. For a few minutes, she was quiet, her lips moving as though in prayer.

Then: she wants to know their name.

Caldera.

Her voice rose. She became animated, using her hands as much as her voice. Tomas translated as she spoke. Yes, there were Calderas in this area. Right in this shop, even. She slapped her hand on the counter. My parents trusted them with credit, she said, and they never let us down. Not like some who took what little you had when your back was turned. She spit at the memory. A family, perhaps two—she thought she recalled uncles and aunties of children roughly her age, though perhaps they only connected a few times a year. The father worked with her father sometimes—they'd be hired to help at a big estate near Jablunkov. Caldera made horseshoes, repaired gates and pots, chimney pieces and wheels for the carriage. There were small houses for the workers, so the family lived there for brief periods. Go to Jablunkov, she says, and ask at the library. The man who works there, Miloŝ, will know—he comes from Malyjavorice. We are to tell him that his Teticka Katka sends us. She's giving us a jar of pickles for him.

I could not stop tears from streaming down my face. Tomas, please thank her for me.

You can thank her, Patrin. You know the words.

So I took her hands in mine this time and said through my tears, Děkuji, Děku. Reaching into the basket on the floor beside her chair, she took out a length of ecru lace and pressed it into my hand.

17

THOSE NIGHTS I slept against her broad back; those mornings I drank coffee bitter with chicory root at her table; those hours we gathered sticks by the river and loaded them into my father's old wagon; those years I saw her only once or twice; those phone calls from my parents' house to her house, the line taut with everything we couldn't say; those cold evenings when I read under the grey and green quilt while she removed seeds from their husks, mended socks with thick wool, fed her stove with pieces of broken cottonwood branch; those hours around her table at the first pomana after my father died, the pastry ring lit from within by a candle; those moments watching her sing her bees into their hives: I never imagined her as a child in these woods, the beeches and oaks heavy with rain, hedgehogs roasting in clay, flavoured with wild sorrel, potatoes in the coals, the horses tethered in their shelter, children being bathed in the running creek and rubbed with rough cloth after, one of them her.

1979

WE FOUND THE market square in Jablunkov with the Catholic church at one end—another town with once lovely buildings now grey and black with soot. A few banners promoting the Party and its activities. Hunched women trudging with shopping bags, one with a large dog on a leash.

The library contained many shelves of books but was empty of patrons. A man with ferocious eyebrows sat at an elevated desk and watched us approach. Tomas greeted him quietly, handing him the pickles. I watched the eyebrows rise, a smile develop and then the two men shaking hands. Then he stepped from behind his desk and shook my hand too. He spoke to me in excellent English.

I'll lock up the library and take you home with me for lunch.

He lived in a small house behind the square, and as we passed the square, he said, This is the Lipky náměsti, because of the lindens. Horse fairs were held here until quite recently. We walked to his home quickly, Tomas guiding the motorcycle, and then Miloŝ helped him prop it up in the entrance hall. I was learning the unspoken directives—leave as few traces of yourself in the public eye as possible. And I had hoarded away the name of the town's square: Lipky.

The kitchen lay at the back of the house, a single window looking out to a narrow garden where neatly pruned fruit trees waited for spring. It would come later to this town in the snowy Beskydy Mountains, though I could see that Miloŝ had already turned the soil in his vegetable beds and had pulled aside the leaf mulch over sprouts he told us were garlic.

And that bird again. Miloŝ, I asked, what kind of bird is that? It was in one of the fruit trees with its tail flitting back and forth, back and forth.

Miloŝ smiled. Ah, it's the wagtail, the pied wagtail. They call it the gypsy bird because where there are people, the wagtail won't be far behind. You'll always find them close to water. (He opened a window, said, Shhhh . . . and we heard the Olza River not far away.) They nest in the broken wall of that building there—he pointed to a crumbling stone building behind his garden. Sure enough, I saw remnants of last year's nest from where we sat.

Once again, I knew I was in the right place. We put out the lunch Mrs. Horakova made for us, and Miloŝ added sausage, and some wrinkled apples he fetched from a room beyond the kitchen—I saw him reach into a barrel for the fruit, brushing straw from them as he brought them to the table. His eyes shone at the sight of the frgál, and he told me that the dark pear paste was most authentic in this part of Moravia.

Your Teticka Katka (he gave a small smile as I said it) suggested you could tell us about the place where my great-grandfather worked sometimes, a big estate near here? And a relative of yours worked there too?

Yes, yes. But it's no longer an estate of course. It's a state farm, worked by the Sisters from the Elizabeth Hospital. You won't be able to visit. I can tell you something about it, yes, but more useful for you, I think, would be to visit the javoriny, the maple pastures maybe you'd say, not far from Malyjavorice, where you were. You go up a rough track from the village, and then you are in the area where the gypsies camped for many many years.

My grandmother's family, do you think?

Almost certainly, he said. And your great-grandfather's metalwork would have been sought after, so I think they would have been regulars at the horse fairs, Lipky náměsti perhaps most of all.

But Tomas says there are almost no Czech gypsies left?

They disappeared of course during the war. We were part of Poland for a time, right here I mean, and many gypsies were transported by the Nazis. And you know about Lety and Hodonin?

I do now, I replied. Though I never learned these things in school.

You wouldn't, he said. No one wanted you to know.

THE SQUARES WITH their leaves, the paths, the stitching like the marks a bird would make, a wagtail following on foot, tail in continual motion, grey, green, the texture a semblance, the pattern a semblance. Hands sewing the secrets of the heart and body, no words to make this record, only scraps of loden wool, worn velvet, one feather, a tiny piece of paper to hold the names of the dead.

1979

WE LEFT THE motorcycle behind a tree when the track became too rough to continue driving. Miloŝ had been quite clear with directions: walk through the mixed forest until you come to an opening, a grassy area, with only an isolated tree here or there. That will be a javorina, first one you come to is on the saddle of hill. It's possible the Calderas camped there—other gypsies did. And about a kilometre along the track, there's another, more hidden. Watch for the glimmer of water through the trees, easier now than in summer, and go left, as though into the forest, and then you'll come to a wide pasture by a small lake. Certainly they camped there. And he'd also suggested we stop in the square and try to imagine the horse fairs, with the gypsies selling pots and kitchen implements, their children dangling their feet in the fountain. We paused by the fountain, and my mind filled with presences, though in reality no one was there in the middle of the day. Walking away from the motorcycle, I shook my head to clear it. Away, the man in the loden cape with children gathered under it for protection from the rain; away, a woman holding two hares by their hind legs.

The trees held a faint premonition of spring, a swelling of buds, a memory of leaves in the high air. Snow still covered the ground in places, which made for slow going.

Is that water? I wasn't sure.

I think, yes.

So we pushed through the snow, and how different these woods were from the west coast of Canada where salal, ferns, Oregon grape and other dense groundcovers made it difficult to walk. I could imagine the trail and the forest in summer, the cool leaves filtering light, birdsong (though I knew we were being observed by a wagtail—I could hear its *chis-wick, chis-wick* as we walked) and perhaps the light footfall of the rare species that still roamed the ancient Beskyds—lynx and wolves, even the occasional bear.

Then we entered the open pasture, fringed with trees, a few low bushes. Some of the snow had melted under the sun's open heat, and although patches of ice still floated on the lake—well, more a pond, a slough—ducks swam around them, mallards, the same ducks I could see any day in Beacon Hill Park.

In snow, the heart-shaped prints of deer. Bird tracks—grouse, they looked like, their angled toes, fine embroidery over a rough surface, the faint gold of their route across the quilt. In a fir tree over by the slough, an azure bird with a high call. From its shape as it suddenly dived into reeds and came up with a tiny fish, I thought it must be a kingfisher, though smaller and more brilliantly coloured than the kingfishers I knew from the ferry dock at Swartz Bay.

I felt as though I knew the place, and I didn't. A clearing in the woods, where my father would have liked to camp, imprinted no doubt by generations of those in his family who also knew a good site, returned to it year after year, left a sign for those following.

(My father made marks on the maps of his friends. Good fishing here, he'd tell them. Or wild blueberries for your morning pancakes. We drove up into Botanie Valley because someone had made a mark on his map in return.) I half-knew the birds but had to be told the most important one of all, the pied wagtail. But it didn't have to be told about me; it found me wherever I stopped in these ancient forests, the towns and villages nearby.

I sat on a stump and pulled out my notebook. I drew the bird tracks, as close to scale as I could manage. I noted the pattern of the trees.

blue kingfisher, curve of fish
        in a long beak
ducks at work on a hidden nest,
        haze of leaves so faintly green
I can see the sky
        through them
I don't fear the voices so let them speak

Tomas was taking photographs. You know Sudek stayed near here, he asked, and I told him yes, Jan told me that. He said there were cabins in the forest. He had a book of photographs, and in some ways I can see the images here. Maybe that's why I recognize the landscape. Though of course there's so much snow!

Have you found what you thought you'd find?

Maybe. Or no, to be honest, but I'm glad we came.

I stood still for what felt like hours but was only minutes, breathing in the cold clean air, listening, listening. Doves cooed, another bird, possibly a grouse, clicking and groaning. Anyone ever here would have heard these sounds.

1979

IN MRS. HORAKOVA'S guesthouse, Tomas in the bed across the room, I fell deep into dreams, the wagtail solemnly taking me to another maple pasture where my great-grandparents sat by a fire, the wheels from their wagon burning, while their children (my grandmother among them) slept the sleep of the dead. This is what people said of sleep, and I never understood what they meant, until then. We were sharing sleep, the living and the dead, that clicking I thought was a grouse in the bushes, and the small owls keeping watch in the beeches.

Several days after we'd arrived in Frenštát, Chavi brought dinner over in iron pots and a basket covered with clean checked cloth. I bring marikla, she said, patting my cheeks again, taking flatbread from her basket, and goja, she said, rubbing her stomach extravagantly as she pointed to a steaming fragrant stew, which Jiři explained were roasted pig guts filled with seasoned potatoes. I don't know if I can eat this, I whispered to Tomas, and you must, he whispered back. I did, and every mouthful tasted delicious. I thought of the pigs feeding under beech trees in autumn, though who raised pigs that way anymore? Who prepared beech mast for animals or humans? For dessert, Chavi had made bobalki, sweet dumplings with a poppy-seed and honey topping. My grandmother made something like this, I told Jiři, who translated for his wife. Sometimes she put sweet plums in them, and we had them with cream. Smetana, said Jiři, closing his eyes in rapture. Smetana, I repeated. Chavi looked so happy to be feeding us at Mrs. Horakova's table, to be offering me not only a taste of her country but of the family who had camped in the javoriny in the early days of the century.

1979

I SENT A POSTCARD to my mother, of the wooden churches of the Beskydy Mountains, and kept my greetings simple. She knew what I was looking for, or at least she understood that I was looking for information about my grandmother. We had talked about it briefly before I left. She wondered if I would do the same for my grandfather one day, and I had to tell her that, at the moment, I could only concentrate on one leafy branch of our family tree. The leaf I'm named for, I said, and she laughed. I so much wanted to name you something more fitting, she said. Diane or Marlene.

I knew what she meant, having spent a few years wanting desperately to be Patty. Anything but Patrin, anything but Szkandery. But in the mountains where my grandmother had been a child, I followed a trail of leaves and knew finally that my name was a blessing.

1979

AGAIN WE BORROWED Mr. Horak's motorcycle, and I lifted the helmet from its new hook by the front door. We had our lunch in Tomas's rucksack—slices of leftover goja and other morsels from Chavi's dinner, dried plums and frgál; the thermos filled with tea. I had my sketch of the quilt and our maps in my notebook tucked into an inner pocket of my jacket.

Nearing Dubová, I grew hyper-alert, though for what exactly, I wasn't certain. Would there be a sign—a dusty patrin on the narrow road, a few leaves tied to a tree?

No, just a small village, houses turned inward, away from the road, high fences concealing their gardens. A shop with a sign on the door: Zavřený. Means "closed," said Tomas over his shoulder. And a pub, also closed. A tiny square, a náměsti, a fountain in the centre—an angel, its wings broken, holding a jug. No water poured from its rim, and from the look of the rust and lichen, no water had tipped from it for years. A cluster of spreading trees, and yes, they were oaks, their dead leaves underfoot. What did this place mean to my great-grandmother? I imagined her being driven from the shop, her children holding her skirts.

I walked around, but no door opened—I mean, of course, in my imagination, as well as those doors that remained firmly shut to me, though later Tomas said that no doubt every move had been observed, and perhaps made note of, to share with an interested party later in the day.

I did find one open door, to the shabby church, and although dark inside, lit only by eight high windows, four on each side, draped with spider webs, it felt somehow welcoming. That smell of old wax and musty pages I remembered from attending Mass with my father a few times in childhood. (My mother, a Presbyterian, made her own accommodations with the Lord, and my father only went to church at Christmas and Easter.) My grandfather was a churchgoer in Beverly but not my grandmother, so it was unlikely this place had meant anything to her family. There might have been parish records, but I found no one to ask. And anyway, did the parishes keep records of gypsies?

Tomas waited outside, leaning against the fountain, one hand keeping the motorbike upright. Anything? he asked, and No, I answered. Nothing here. Tomas had told me earlier that I wouldn't be allowed to see any of the police records from the area. Much secrecy surrounded the Roma and how they were accounted for and dealt with. One day these will open up, he said with a kind of fierce optimism, and I wanted to believe him.

So we continued along the road that skirted the mountain, Radhošt', which towered over the countryside. We saw little traffic. An occasional Skoda, another motorcycle, its driver raising a hand in greeting as he passed us going the other way.

Could we stop, I asked, because it seemed to me that the road was curving around a particular grove of trees in a way that felt familiar. (My hands on the loden leaves and their black velvet shadows, the grey wool pathways between them . . . .) The bike wobbled a bit on its bent kickstand, and we spread out my jacket on the ground to orient ourselves with both maps. On the trees, the leaves were just unfolding, and I saw that they were beech leaves—we had a tattered copy of *The Trees of Moravia and Silesia* to help us, me finding the right drawing and Tomas reading the botanical description. On the map, we saw that a river curved nearby and that we were just a few kilometres from Velký Buková.

I left Tomas with the motorbike and walked into the trees. If they had anything to do with me, I thought I would feel it.

Nothing.

But then I went farther, the ground almost park-like, crunchy underfoot with leaves from the previous autumn, and I came to an opening, a small meadow of rich green grass emerging from the brown grass of winter. Light came through the fringe of trees like a Sudek photograph, touching grass, leaves, the ancient contours of the ground. The world began to shimmer. I felt faint, as though the planet had tipped, and everything was slant. And I knew I wasn't alone. I turned. No one. A hare near the meadow's edge, frogs ardent in the distance, and then a small black-and-white bird on the low branch of a tree. A wagtail, looking like a smaller cousin to the magpies that haunted my grandmother's garden in Edmonton. It began to sing.

A man came through the trees with a few straggly sheep, surprised to find me there and even more surprised to discover that I couldn't speak Czech. Luckily Tomas arrived too, wondering where I was. The two of them spoke in that tentative way of strangers meeting and wondering about intentions, one (or two, if you counted me) perhaps trespassing. Tomas nodded towards me, and the man looked at me curiously. His sheep took the opportunity to graze. They wore bells, each sounding a slightly different note, and when they reached down to the grass and then lifted their heads, their bells rang sweetly. They reminded me of the goats near Chora Skafion, and if I knew more about music, I'd try to make a little composition using the phrasing of bells. I carried my sealstone in my pocket, and I touched it briefly in memory.

Tomas fished our thermos of tea out of his rucksack and poured some into the tin cup. He offered it to the man first. We watched as he drank. Děku, he said. Tomas introduced me, and the man shook my hand. Vaclav, he pointed to his chest. And he made a big sweep with his arms. Cikán, he said to me, indicating the meadow and its fringe of trees.

Tomas helped us both by talking to Vaclav. He translated for me as quickly as he could. He told me this was a campsite for Roma people—he uses the Czech word for gypsies—until the compulsory settlement in 1958. They'd come for many years. His own grandparents remember them. And Patrin, here's the thing. The people in Velký Buková called this Malý Bukova. Little beech. There's a creek over there—he pointed—running down to the main river so there was water. Grass for the horses. Beechnuts for the pigs in fall. The bonfire where the police burned the cart-wheels was there—he pointed to a depression in the earth, as grassy now as any other area. The gypsies had to walk to the train station so they could be taken to their new homes. Or they rode horses, which were kept tethered outside the flats. When Vaclav laughed suddenly, slapping his knees, Tomas whispered that the townspeople may not have liked the gypsies but they loved the horse manure for their gardens.

The man kept talking, intrigued to meet a foreigner—not many tourists found their way to this part of Czechoslovakia, so I was a novelty. He was taking his sheep to pasture farther up the mountain, and maybe he should get them there because the day only had so many hours, but then he casually said something to Tomas that caused Tomas to grin broadly. He shook the man's hand, and then waited until we'd said good bye, watching Vaclav clap his hands and use his long stick to tap at the sheeps' legs to get them moving. Na shledanou, he called, na shledanou, and we called back to him: na shledanou! Goodbye!

Tomas took my hand and squeezed it hard. Patrin, he said to be sure to see the gypsy graveyard. It's in the trees about half a kilometre that way.

1979

I SENT A POSTCARD to Jan, an image of the pagan god Radegast, associated with hospitality (I hoped he'd deduce that Tomas was as helpful as Jan had promised he'd be), watching from high on his perch on Radhošt', and I wrote only two sentences: Wonderful hiking in the Beskydy Mountains. The map is too dated to be truly useful, but the scenery is beautiful.

1979

A LOW FENCE MADE of loose stones piled on one another. An iron gate, rough with rust, and 27 mounds, I thought—I counted as carefully as I could, but the uneven ground was deceptive.

Some mounds had small arrangements of plastic flowers and photographs of the deceased anchored with pebbles to the rough slabs that served as headstones. Those beneath were remembered—one bouquet of flowers still had a price tag attached to it, a recent offering.

A wagtail again, flicking its tail. Do you think it's following us, Tomas?

I have no idea, he replied. Preoccupied, he was taking photographs with an ancient camera. I had an Instamatic with me and pulled it out of the pocket of my anorak, handed it to him. Use mine, I said. You can keep the film, I have more. You don't need to use your own for this.

But no, no, he waved my camera away. My friend will develop my film, he said. Remember I told you that even the walls have ears? Well, photo shops do too—and I can imagine what would happen to film I took in which showed images of gypsy graveyards.

I went from one grave to the next. Most had no names but marks of some sort, softened now with moss and age. No dates that I could see. The wagtail inclined its head. Who was who in this community of the dead?

Tomas, the poem Barbora translated for me? Can you remember the English?

He pulled out his notebook. I've been making a translation for you to help you take it to heart, he said, smiling.

> Don't fear the voices, there's a lot of them,
> the wind has combed the grass
> the past few days....

I interrupted him. The thing is, Tomas, I do hear them. Or I hear something. Murmuring, it sounds like murmuring. Maybe it's just wind or squirrels or hedgehogs in the undergrowth, but it sounds like voices.

This is what you wanted, I think?

But I don't know what they're saying.

Funny woman, he commented. You don't speak Czech or Romani, so how could you know?

But I didn't think the heart had a specific language, though I didn't say this.

1978

I LIKED TO VISIT a little record store in a courtyard between View Street and Yates Street, and once I began earning money at the bookshop, I'd go there on my lunch hour, in search of music to remind me I wasn't alone in the world. The shop had only a small section of albums that were not classical—clearly the proprietor's passion—and in fact he always had something playing, Pachelbel one day or Vivaldi another. If I asked about the music swirling through the cosy room, the owner's face would light up, and he'd talk for ages about the composer. My own face lit up too as the notes echoed the owner's words, a sweet counterpoint in that little store.

One day I found a recording of gypsy music from Bulgaria and Macedonia. I knew that the Romani people didn't observe political or geographical borders, so I assumed that their music wouldn't either. Some of the musicians' names were Greek, others sounded more Slavic. But the music was vibrant in any language, and I heard phrasing I recognized, passages that could have been Nestor on the terrace those mornings in Chania. So the zurna, yes, and other instruments I didn't recognize. But after looking at the liner notes, I determined that the sound like a bagpipe must have been the gaida, made of goatskin, and that the hauntingly familiar sound of the lyra, which I recognized from the music sessions in Chania, was in fact the gadulka, which went back to the same Byzantine roots as the lyra. There was also a tambura, not unlike the mandolins played by contemporary folk musicians.

In my apartment, I played this album until it warped from the heat of sunlight shining right onto the turntable—I saw no point in putting the record away because I'd only take it out again an hour or two later. I needed to hear those songs coming into my life from the other side of the world, as if coded messages from a place I'd never been. (Kardia mou, I haven't forgotten your body in the morning light, your oval face, your eyes looking into mine as we drank our coffee at the table overlooking the old harbour.) I no longer hurt to think of him, but the music made me nostalgic, wistful, and I wondered if anyone would ever truly love me.

1979

I FOUND NOTHING DEFINITE. No names or obvious markers to say, These are yours. Whatever is left of them, this is your patrimony, the roots of your family tree tangling under the earth. A tattered nest in one of the beech trees—a reminder of Tas? And everywhere, Adamu, the earth rich with him. Florica would emerge each spring, like Persephone, a wild scattering of flowers in the soft grass. And if they believed in God—as my grandmother did, in her own way—then Fifika was his blessing, as roots love the rain or new leaves the sunlight. I could hear bees in the beech catkins and wondered if those children had ever been sent by their parents to follow the bees to their hives, hidden in hollow trees (the linden was best), standing back while their father reached in with his long gloved hands for the dripping combs.

The quilt's crooked sashing—how much I had hoped those winding lengths were specific roads; and the faded golden tracks would lead me to . . . well, what, exactly? I'd walked in the meadows where my family had camped. I'd seen the fountain at Lipky náměsti where children played in the spray under the spreading shade of the lindens. I had searched the graveyard where some of the children might have been buried, or if not them, others whose lines of connection would lead in a meandering way—cousins, aunts, half-brothers or sisters—to my great-grandmother and my great-grandfather who were probably buried somewhere in Canada. My father had tried to find them, but now I would take my turn. I'd try harder. I decided that the quilt was indeed a map but only for my great-grandmother, who needed to commemorate her own lost children, the places they'd known in sunlight and in snow, and the roads they'd travelled on foot or on horseback.

I crumbled a little bobalki, scattered a bit of goja, crying as I pressed the crumbs into the earth. Birds would eat it, but the gesture seemed appropriate. I sang the lullaby I'd loved best as a child, "The Water Is Wide," and the words seemed as true as anything I could tell them, though perhaps it was not what one should sing to the dead, who no longer had choices to make about love or anything else. But love doesn't always involve choice. My grandmother and grandfather, kissing under the lifeboats on the *Mount Temple*—did they choose one another or were they simply drawn together as rivers find the sea? I didn't think the people buried in the cemetery would have chosen me to carry what remained of their promise, their hope. I had a job with no true future. I'd been afraid to hold my father's hands while he died. I was selfish. I did so few things well. But I was what was left of them, and for this reason I cried and sang.

The water is wide, I cannot cross o'er.
And neither have I wings to fly.
Give me a boat that can carry two,
And both shall row, my love and I.

It was quiet among the graves, the trees with their branches ready to burst into leaf. I sang for the dead children and for my young great-grandparents kissing and for my own first love:

I leaned my back up against a young oak,
Thinking he were a trusty tree
But first he bended and then he broke...

It was strange how love came into my life, not in the expected way, aunts and uncles around a table, a joyous celebration, or a young man reaching for my hand in a darkened movie theatre, the caress of his thumb on mine making my skin tingle, but this, the knowledge of my family's past entering my whole body as naturally as oxygen and someone, unlikely, unlooked for, who helped it happen. Not a man playing his zurna to the night on a ferry to Crete but someone waiting by the edge of the graveyard for me to turn to him so he could say that it was time to leave, because Mr. Horak would want his motorcycle for the evening. I walked out of the graveyard without looking back.

SOME NIGHTS WERE almost too warm for my quilt, the nights when the apartment's erratic radiators poured forth heat. But I kept it pulled up to my chin, hoping that its secrets would penetrate my skin like a faint sooty tattoo. In the morning, I woke to the stale smell of woodsmoke and old wool, the chaff of the rough backing where it rubbed my bare sleeping shoulders, exactly like the touch of my grandmother's hands—lanolin and chapped skin. I imagined the interior of the wagon would smell exactly like this—the wool and smoke in the bedding, the clothing, the hair of the children who would have been my great aunts and uncles.

1979

WHAT MADE ME recognize love in the gypsy graveyard? I no longer pined for Nestor, and hadn't for ages; still, I hadn't expected to feel what I felt when I climbed on the back of the motorcycle to wrap my arms around Tomas's back, the scent of his hair as potent as wine. Back at Mrs. Horakova's guesthouse, changing out of my muddy jeans into my clean pair in our shared room while Tomas waited outside in the hall, I knew suddenly that I loved him. What he had done for me in the time I'd spent with him had been nothing short of remarkable. He met a total stranger at the train station, slept on the floor so I could have a bed, led me through the grey streets of his forbidding city and made me see it as it could truly be, given time and will. He had taken me to the very place, at least what I hoped was the place, where my ancestors had been buried so many years ago, forgotten in their otherness by everyone except an old woman in a dusty shop and the wagtails in the javoriny.

When I opened the door, holding my muddy pants, he took them from me and said he would shake them out in the back yard. I followed him there, and together we hung them on the clothesline, then continued into the back lane where I took his right hand in my left, stroked his thumb with mine. Tomas, I began, wondering how I would tell him that I loved him. We kept walking.

Kept walking out of the town, along a road that became a track, along the track until we came to a small grove of trees—beeches, oaks, maples, lindens. Meeting each other's eyes, we stepped across the ditch and into the grove. I heard the quilt sketch crackle as I lay back on my jacket. We had not yet kissed.

NOTES

PATRIN BEGAN AS an unexpected detour from a road I was travelling toward what I hoped would be the heart of my paternal grandmother's past. In looking for my grandmother, who came to Canada from a small village in the Beskydy Mountains in what is now Moravia, I also found the presence of the Roma of the Czech Republic and Slovakia. Sometimes unsettling, sometimes intriguing, their stories made me want to know more about their history in the landscapes where I was also finding traces of my own family. My grandmother was not a Roma woman. This story isn't hers, or mine, although there are many elements in the novella that come from my background, my early travels, my father's childhood in Beverly, Alberta, and the Central European diaspora that my father's family belonged to.

I read many books about the lives of Roma people and Slavik farmers in the Austro-Hungarian Empire and visited some archives, notably the Museum of Romani Culture in Brno, CR. I found stories about hardship, bureaucratic difficulties, documents badly translated, children lost from memory, work camps, and the resilience of the human spirit. Some of these stories were specific to the Roma and some applied to my own family.

ACKNOWLEDGEMENTS

PETR KOPECKY AND Lenka Szczerba for taking me to Horni Lomna. Katka Prajznerova for discussion about specific trees as well as so much else. Anik See and Angelica Pass for reading an earlier version of *Patrin*. At Mother Tongue: Mona Fertig for her enthusiastic dedication to books; Pearl Luke for gracious and intelligent editorial guidance; Diana Hayes for knowing exactly which tree should hold the patrin; and Setareh Ashrafologhalai for a beautiful design. And at home: John Pass for everything.